Russell Bates · Simon J. Ortiz
Leslie Marmon Silko · Louise Erdrich
Gerald Vizenor · Mary Whitebird

Native American Short Stories

Edited
by Hans Günter Mischkowski

Ernst Klett Schulbuchverlag

Herausgegeben von Hans Günter Mischkowski, Göttingen.

Acknowledgements

Russell Bates, "Rite of Encounter." © 1973 by Mercury Press, Inc. Reprinted from *The Magazine of Fantasy and Science Fiction* by permission of the author.

Simon J. Ortiz, "Pennstuwehniyaahtsi: Quuti's Story" from *Fightin': New and Collected Stories,* Chicago: Thunder's Mouth Press, 1983. Reprinted by permission.

Leslie Marmon Silko, "Lullaby," first published in *Chicago Review* 1974, copyright © 1974, is reprinted by permission of the author.

Louise Erdrich, "Snares." Copyright © 1987 by *Harper's Magazine.* All rights reserved. Reprinted from the May issue by special permission.

Gerald Vizenor, "Marleen American Horse" from *Wordarrows,* Minneapolis: University of Minnesota Press, 1978, is reprinted by permission of the publisher.

Mary Whitebird, "Ta-Na-E-Ka." Copyright © 1973 by Scholastic Inc. Reprinted and recorded by permission of Scholastic Inc.

The cassette accompanying this book contains the stories by Simon J. Ortiz, Leslie Marmon Silko, Gerald Vizenor and Mary Whitebird (Klettnummer 57935).

1. Auflage 1 5 4 3 2 1 | 1995 94 93 92 91

Die letzte Zahl bezeichnet das Jahr dieses Druckes. Alle Drucke dieser Auflage können im Unterricht nebeneinander benutzt werden.

Redaktion: Dr. Hartmut K. Selke, Verlagsredakteur

Druck: Gutmann & Co., Heilbronn
ISBN 3-12-579330-0

Contents

Introduction

The American Indian and the American West have always fascinated both youngsters and adults in Germany. Whereas fiction about the American Indians written in Germany (Karl May comes to mind) has largely tended to idealize them, Western movies for a long time demonized them. Thus contradictory clichés were created that linger on to this day.

If we want to obtain firsthand knowledge of "Native Americans" (the term most frequently used these days), we must turn either to historical texts – both literary and documentary – or to contemporary literature written in English by American Indians. It stands to reason that the latter genre is much more accessible to students in the EFL classroom.

During the last three decades Native Americans have published a large number of poems, novels and short stories drawing our attention to the hardships their people have endured throughout American history up to the present day. Much of this literature, poems and novels in particular, consists of highly sophisticated texts blending old tribal elements (taken from the oral tradition) and modern literary techniques such as the free association of ideas and the stream of consciousness. N. Scott Momaday's novel *House Made of Dawn* (1968) and Leslie Marmon Silko's *Ceremony* (1977), for example, are outstanding literary achievements.

Obviously, short stories, such as those anthologized here, are better suited to introduce students to contemporary Native American literature. The stories printed here have been selected with two criteria in mind. First, the students get to know some of the most prominent contemporary writers of the genre, such as Leslie Marmon Silko, Simon J. Ortiz, Gerald Vizenor and Louise Erdrich. Second, the stories deal with important historical and contemporary aspects of the Native American experience. Thus "Rite of Encounter" portrays the fatal clash between Indians and whites, and "Pennstuwehniyaahtsi: Quuti's Story" shows the problems resulting from an enforced acculturation intended to lead to total assimilation. The conflict between traditionalists and "progressive" Indians is satirized in "Snares". In order to further illustrate the crucial choice between the preservation of traditional values and the adjustment to the American way of life "Ta-Na-E-Ka" has been included here. This story, in advocating total integration and assimilation, obviously mirrors the whites' point of view. The answers given by other authors are different: "Lullaby", which tells the story of a Navajo working for a white rancher, and "Marleen American Horse", about life on the urban reservation in Minneapolis, show the problems resulting from the Indians' estrangement from their own traditional concept of life. But they also hint at solutions to the Native American's identity conflict: ethnic pride and the reliance on traditional beliefs and value systems that are indispensable for survival.

Thus the aims of Native American authors are dual: On the one hand they give the Indians' side of the story, they want to reach their own ethnic group in order to define their own Native American consciousness. On the other hand they present their people's plight to a white reading public. The identity problems of American Indians who are torn between two cultures tend to "strike a responsive chord in teenagers who are in search of self-realization" (Anna Lee Stensland, *Literature by and about the American Indian,* Urbana, 1979). In addition, the Indian view of the relationship between people and nature is likely to appeal to young people many of whom call into question the materialism of the success-oriented society they live in.

Russell Bates

Rite of Encounter

In the third week of his fasting, Singing-owl found the white men.

The young Kiowa awakened that morning to lilting daybreak calls of birds. Rain had fallen in the night; his buffalo robe was soaked and smelly; his buckskin shirt and leggings were clammy wet. He was miserable. A chill wind blew in under the overhanging rocks. Singing-owl shivered, almost forgetting the receding hunger pangs. Almost ....

At last the sun warmed the rocks around him. Singing-owl sat up wearily, hoping that this new day would finally bring him the vision. He dried his long black hair and braided it loosely on the left side. Then he stared for a long while downward from the rocky cleft. The hillside was unchanging: scattered clumps of scrub oaks, moss-grown boulders, thick yellow-green grass and black soil. Hillsides beyond bore the same colors and shapes.

Singing-owl had dreamed sometime before dawn. Of deer and clouds and fishes and snow .... But the dream had not been the vision he was seeking. When that came, he would speak with spirits and come away with pieces of their wisdom. The wisdom, in songs and chants and riddles, would be his power as a warrior and as a man.

At least that was what the medicine man promised to him. But how much longer did he have to wait? The moon had been just past full when Singing-owl started his fast; soon, it would be full once again.

Singing-owl thought of the medicine man who slept warm at the camp and had no want of food or clothing.

That toothless, half-blind old man! I hope he got bloated on the meat I gave him!

The hunger pangs increased at the mention of food. Singing-owl leaned

rite a solemn ceremony (often a religious one) – **encounter** meeting; fight – 1 **fasting** period of time spent without eating anything – 2 **lilting** melodious – 4 **buckskin** soft leather made from deerskin – **leggings** a covering for the legs – **clammy** cold and sticky – **chill** cold – 6 **to recede** [rɪ'si:d] to go back; *here:* to become weaker – **pangs** strong feeling of pain – 9 **to braid** flechten – 10 **cleft** crack in the ground – 11 **scrub oaks** small oak trees (Eichen) – **boulder** big piece of rock – 16 **chant** a sacred song – 22 **want** lack – 23 **bloated** swollen, fat (aufgedunsen)

over and pulled a small deerskin parcel from a crack in the rocks. Wrapped inside was a handful of pounded dried meat mixed with suet. He smelled it for a long time, then closed his eyes and tried to swallow. He put the meat away again, feeling very guilty.

At length he forced himself to leave the cleft. When he stood, dizziness and nausea made him stagger. He leaned back against the rocks, momentarily unable to see. His arms and legs tingled and a cramp twisted the muscles in his side. Then the white sparkles faded from before his eyes.

Water. Must get water.

Singing-owl made his way carefully down the hill; the going was harder than the day before. He could no longer jump from boulder to boulder and instead squeezed between them. Sharp rocks hurt his feet through wet moccasins.

The slope leveled off, and Singing-owl sat on the ground to catch his breath. He glanced up the hill; it didn't seem any higher than he remembered. But now he regretted having passed by other, more gentle slopes.

I chose my suffering spot well. But will I be able to climb it again?

He followed a deer trail and walked listlessly among the trees. Twice he stumbled over tree roots. Another time he brushed against a tree and grabbed it desperately to keep from falling. He stopped and looked around.

Is this the right trail to the river? It's so long. I'm lost!

Singing-owl left the trail and headed away across the clearing. The thick grass slowed him to a stumbling pace. Then he smelled water and knew the river was close.

When he reached its muddy bank, he fell to his knees and threw himself forward to drink. The river was cool and slightly muddied. But the water made him feel better. He washed his face, then stripped off his buckskins to wash the many bruised cuts on his arms, chest and back. His frenzied thrashing against the rocks the evening before had gained him nothing but exhausted sleep; the self-tortures had not made him worthy of the vision. At last, Singing-owl slipped into the water and washed himself vigorously. Some

2 **pounded** made into powder – **suet** ['su:ɪt] Talg – 5 **at length** after a long time – **dizziness** unsteadiness, a feeling that everything is going round in circles – 6 **nausea** ['nɔ:sjə] feeling of sickness – **to stagger** to walk, move unsteadily – 7 **to tingle** prickeln – 8 **sparkle** flash of light – **to fade** *here:* to disappear slowly – 12 **to squeeze** to force s.th. or s.o. between two objects which are very close together – 14 **to level off** to become less steep – 18 **listless** weak, tired – 28 **bruised** [bru:zd] injured by a blow – **frenzied** ['frenzɪd] very excited – **to thrash** to beat – 31 **vigorous** strong, with much energy

of the fatigue, muscle aches, and light-headedness flowed away with the sandy mud he used for scrubbing.

Then he lay against a log at the water's edge; the river current soothed his body. It was a struggle to stay awake.

A dog barked. Singing-owl sat up and listened. Again. Close by. Upstream.

He crawled out of the water, grabbed his buckskins, and listened again. The barking broke into howls. He scrambled up the bank into bushes and made his way toward the sound, at once curious and afraid.

In this isolated land, no other tribes roamed. A dog meant white men.

Singing-owl paused to put on his buckskins. Then he crept ahead through the bushes: cautious, patient, silent. A few moments later, he reached the edge of a clearing and could see the camp, the dog, and the white men.

The dog was tied to a tree. One white man lay beside a long-dead fire. Another sat against a tree, his arms limp, his head fallen forward to his chest. A third lay sprawled on the riverbank, his head and one arm in the water. All were dressed in dirty gray and brown clothes, with boots scuffed and mud-caked.

A breeze fluttered the leaves of cottonwoods around the clearing; it also brought Singing-owl a whiff of decay. The men were dead.

The dog sensed Singing-owl and barked louder, leaping to the limit of the rope. Singing-owl stood up slowly, then walked into the camp. The dog retreated a little but kept up its barking. Singing-owl noticed a broken rope between two trees; horses had long since pulled free and wandered off.

He stopped at the body lying beside the ashes. The dead man lay face-down, a blanket across his legs. Singing-owl bent down, picked up a fine pistol; it was fully loaded, with light, circular tracings along the barrel. Perhaps there were other weapons.

Singing-owl turned to the dog. It was brown and white spotted; its fur was matted and the mouth was dirty. Starving and dying of thirst, it had been eating mud.

Singing-owl put the gun in his shirt and hunted through the men's packs. He found hardtack biscuits and dried meat. He also found metal cans but

1 **fatigue** [fə'ti:g] state of being very tired, exhausted – **light-headedness** dizziness – 3 **current** the movement of water in a river – **to soothe** [su:ð] to ease pain – 7 **to scramble** to climb – 11 **cautious** ['kɔ:ʃəs] careful – 12 **clearing** area without trees in a forest (Lichtung) – 15 **sprawled** with his arms and legs spread out – 16 **scuffed** worn out – **mud-caked** covered with dried mud – 18 **cottonwood** *(A.E.)* a poplar tree growing in the U.S. (Pappel) – 19 **whiff** smell in the air (lasting only for a short while) – **decay** [dɪ'keɪ] Verwesung – 29 **matted** verfilzt – 32 **hardtack biscuits** Schiffszwieback

discarded them because their markings were meaningless. He looked with longing at the food. But another nudge of guilt made him throw it to the dog.

It sniffed the morsels suspiciously, then began to eat in great gulps.

Singing-owl sighed, then picked up a small pot to get water. He shivered as he passed the man by the tree. At the riverbank he noticed something strange as he bent to fill the pot. The dead man lying there was covered with sores.

He looked closer. The hand that lay out of the water was almost raw; crusted yellow ooze edged what little skin remained on its back. He looked at the face. The sores there had ragged white strings that waved in the flowing water. Singing-owl filled the pot quickly and stepped away.

The dog drank the water and wagged its tail. Then it looked up at him, expectant. Singing-owl reached out carefully, untied the rope. The dog brushed against him, happy.

"What killed your people, dog?" Singing-owl said, not truly breaking the ban against speaking to anyone.

The dog shook its head and barked. Its tail slapped against Singing-owl's legs.

"That was a bad way to meet death. Maybe I'd better not stay here any longer." He skirted wide of the man sitting at the tree. Yes, the sores were there. He didn't bother turning over the man under the blanket.

Singing-owl remembered the pistol; he took it out with a trembling hand and dropped it. The dog walked with him away from the camp, then stopped.

Singing-owl looked back. "Going to stay here, yes? I wouldn't be able to keep you anyway. Hope you find something to eat. ..." He brushed away the obvious and horrible thought, heading back into the hills.

When evening came, Singing-owl made a small fire and began his chanting prayers. The wind blew warm over the rocky cleft; stars were glistening in the dying film of twilight. Surely the strange events of the day were signs that the vision was coming. The robes that hid things to come would be lifted and ...

Singing-owl found himself repeating the words of the medicine man and was disgusted. He waited. Nothing. The air turned cool and the fire slowly fell away.

1 **to discard** to throw away – 2 **with longing** with desire, with a great wish – **nudge** gentle push; *here:* a feeling – 3 **morsel** very small piece of food – **gulp** [gʌlp] swallowing movement – 6 **sore** diseased spot of skin – 8 **crusted** having become hard on the outside – **ooze** [u:z] slime, liquid found on open wounds – 9 **ragged** ['rægɪd] badly torn – 19 **to skirt** to pass around s.o. or s.th. – 20 **to bother** to take the trouble – 28 **twilight** faint light from the sun below the horizon – 29 **robe** an article of clothing, usually long and loose

Where is it? The medicine man is a liar! But what of all the other warriors who claim power from a vision?

He sat quietly, then decided to fast for only a few more days. If no vision came, he would go back to the Kiowas. He'd have to tell them something; exactly what, he did not know.

But he would repay the medicine man for many days of discomfort. Singing-owl's brow wrinkled as he half frowned, half smiled. His reputation for playing pranks and outwitting his tribesmen was to gain yet another distinction. He would do nothing harmful, to be sure, just a few tricks to upset the old man. Such as: giving him skunk bones if he asked for weasel, hawk meat if he asked for prairie bird, or putting green sticks in his firewood. Singing-owl wanted to laugh, but he couldn't.

He noticed the fire and started to add more wood. But he felt warm enough; in fact, he felt almost too warm. He touched his face: hot.

Perhaps I'm tired. All right. I am tired.

He lay down to sleep. He remembered the white men and their sores. though he really didn't want to. Something had killed them. Quickly. Quietly. He tried to think of other things. The vision. The many tricks he had played. Gray Bear's daughters. A running hunt through trees after a deer. But nothing forced the image of the dead men from the edge of his sight. Finally, he fell asleep, feeling warmer than before.

Singing-owl opened his eyes. The sun was high above the hills. He lay quietly and listened to his body. All was well, apparently. Relieved, he sat up, yawned and stretched. He pushed the buffalo robe away and started to get up.

The thing sat a short distance away, watching him. Singing-owl stared, unable to move further. It was shaped like a man. But it wasn't a man.

It was a mass of raw flesh. With a body, and arms and legs, and a head. No skin or hair; just endless running sores. It appeared to be looking at him, but its face was featureless, red, open flesh. Yellow fluids trickled from over its entire body; wet streams ran down the rock on which it sat.

Singing-owl crawled backward, pressed himself against the rocks, eyes wide.

A ghost? Is it a white man's ghost? Or is … is that the vision?

7 **brow** [braʊ] forehead – 8 **prank** trick, practical joke – **to outwit** to defeat by a clever trick – 10 **skunk** Stinktier – 30 **featureless** with no recognizable markings or expression – **fluid** Flüssigkeit

He choked on the words: "Are you one of the spirits? Have … have you come because I am worthy?"

It moved, raised an arm, touched its chest. In a thick watery voice, it said, "I am Black Smallpox. And I wish to walk with you."

Singing-owl almost fainted. He stared at it, tried to speak.

But the creature spoke first. "Do not be afraid. I will not harm you. I only wish to go with you to the Kiowas." It stood, and the yellow streams ran down its legs. "Yes, we will walk together to your people."

Singing-owl thought quickly, blinking. It surely was not the vision. Or was it perhaps the vision after all, somehow spoiled by white man's evil? Yes, the white men. Their sores. *Death.*

"No!" he said, feeling for a loose rock. "You came with the white men! You killed them! And now you want to kill. …" He found a rock and threw it. Smallpox wavered like a reflection in water, then suddenly was standing a short distance further away. The rock clattered harmlessly to the ground.

Smallpox stepped closer. "Come. Let us go."

Singing-owl sprang away suddenly and clambered down the hillside. He ran, stumbled, fell, crawled, slid over boulders, ran again. When he reached flatter ground, he broke into a run and didn't look back. He staggered and almost tripped several times. He ran past trees, over hills, down gullies, into grass and bare ground.

At last he ran, stumbled, ran into a narrow valley. He fell, gasping and crying. He landed on his face and hands at the edge of a rain water pool. He lay beside a boulder and a small bush. He tried to crawl, but fell back. His body shook and shivered, though sweat coated him. Then his breathing slowed and he raised himself on one arm.

Singing-owl heard wailing and moaning, but very faint. Then he saw people reflected in the pool. They were Kiowas; ragged, wet sores covered their arms and faces. The wailing reflections reached for him, crying louder.

Singing-owl jerked himself backward and pushed dirt into the pool with his feet. Something stood at the limit of his side vision; he turned and saw Smallpox standing beside the bush.

It stepped toward him. "Why did you stop? We are going to the Kiowas, are we not? The sooner we get there, the better it will please me."

1 **to choke** to be unable to breathe – 10 **to spoil** to ruin, to make useless – 14 **to waver** to move unsteadily – 15 **to clatter** to make a noise while falling – 20 **to trip** to fall – **gully** channel formed by rainwater – 22 **to gasp** to take in breath quickly – 25 **to coat** to cover – 27 **to wail** to cry, to complain in a loud voice – **to moan** to make a low sound of pain – **faint** weak – 30 **to jerk** to make a short sudden movement

Singing-owl scrambled up, backed away in a low crouch. “No! I won’t take you! You have no place here! Go away!”

It raised a hand. “We must go. The day grows long.”

Singing-owl turned and ran again.

He climbed a cliff. Smallpox walked to the edge above him before he reached the top.

He ran over the plateau and dove from more than treetop height into a lake. Smallpox stood atop the beaver lodge when Singing-owl swam toward the dam.

He hid in a box canyon. Smallpox was standing behind him near the sheer rock face. Singing-owl quickly set a grass fire by striking stones together. The flames swept into the canyon, swirling with smoke, trapping Smallpox. But when Singing-owl ran into a forest, Smallpox stepped from behind a tree to meet him.

Through the rest of the day Singing-owl ran, set traps, ran again. But he could neither outrun nor outwit Smallpox; it was always there when he stopped. Night fell and Singing-owl found he could run no more.

He sat on the top of a grassy hill and watched as Smallpox walked slowly toward him. Light from a nearly full moon flashed in white sparks from the dripping liquids.

I have lost. I have no more tricks. Yet ....

Singing-owl thought hurriedly, formed a plan, then hung his head as Smallpox stopped beside him. “All right,” he said. “We will go to the Kiowas.”

Somewhere, Singing-owl felt a flicker of hope.

The lodges were quiet; moonlight revealed a score or more of them built at the base of a tree-lined hill. The main campfire was low. Camp dogs roamed in the spaces between the lodges. Sentries stood unmoving at long intervals around the village.

At a distance, Singing-owl circled the camp quietly. Smallpox walked with him.

1 **crouch** an almost sitting position with the knees bent and the body bent down to the ground – 7 **dove** *A.E.:* past tense of to dive – 8 **beaver lodge** Biberbau – 10 **box** small, evergreen tree (Buchsbaum) – **sheer** very steep, vertical – 12 **to swirl** to move along in circles – 22 **to hang one’s head** to turn one’s head to the ground when ashamed or without hope – 26 **lodge** small house, hut – **a score** a group or set of 20 – 27 **to roam** to walk without aim – 28 **sentry** guard

At the far end of the camp, a woman came out of a lodge and threw bones on the ground. The dogs ran toward her and began fighting over the meal.

Singing-owl saw his chance and boldly walked in among the lodges where there was no sentry. Then he stopped and abruptly turned to Smallpox. "We are here. Now will you let me go? I am ashamed."

It stepped forward and regarded the circle of lodges. "Not just yet. There is still something you must do. Come."

He followed it, glancing from side to side, nervous. Smallpox led him to a large deerskin bag that was supported by crossed poles.

"This water," it said, standing very close to him and pointing. "Spit into it."

Singing-owl only stared, not understanding.

"I said, spit into this water."

He stepped to the bag, opened a flap near the top, and spat.

"Again. That will do it. You are free."

Singing-owl moved back. "Free?"

Smallpox turned away. "Your usefulness is at an end." It sat down, still with its back to him; the open flesh gleamed wetly in the moonlight. "You will not understand, but I will tell you anyway. There are but a few I cannot kill. You are one. But I still lived inside you and thus was my purpose served. Leave me."

Singing-owl pretended to walk toward a lodge near large shade trees. "Yes," he said, looking back. "I must go to my lodge. My family will be glad to see me."

But when Smallpox was no longer in sight, Singing-owl ran for the trees. Two dogs ran after him, barking. A sentry shouted and more dogs ran after him. Singing-owl reached the shadows and ran out of the camp. He lost his pursuers quickly.

I'm free. I'm free! And the Pawnees are no friends to the Kiowas! They deserve Smallpox!

Dawn found Singing-owl far away from the Pawnee camp. When he was sure no one followed, he trapped a rabbit and ate his first meal in twenty days. His stomach ached a little when he set out again. But he was still happy at finally outwitting Smallpox.

He laughed. What a tale he would tell of his vision when he reached the Kiowas!

3 **bold** brave, courageous – 9 **pole** long straight wooden stick – 14 **flap** opening of the deerskin bag – 28 **pursuer** [– '– –] s.o. who chases and tries to catch another person

He was almost there when he heard wailing. He stopped and looked around frantically. Nothing else could be seen on the rolling plains except grasses moving in the wind. Then the wailing faded to be replaced by a laughing taunt. It was the voice of Smallpox.

"Where are you?" Singing-owl said, turning in circles. "You cannot be here! I outwitted you!"

"I told you, but you did not understand. We still walk together. I am a part of you. I will be with you always. You cannot get rid of me!" And the laughing began again.

Then Singing-owl knew the laughing came from inside him. He clutched at himself, tore at his own flesh, and screamed.

The laugh rolled on, unstopping.

The cleft of rocks offered little protection from the raging thunderstorm. Singing-owl huddled under his buffalo robe and watched the storm. Lightning split trees on far hills and flashed the night away for brief moments. Thunder snapped down from the clouds and shook the ground. Rain splashed on Singing-owl's face and ran in pools under him.

He prayed, asked the mercy of the spirits. Small things came back to him: a boy's game with a willow hoop; his mother and stories and songs and gentle scoldings; the self-tortures that had declared him a man; the smiling, teasing daughter of Gray Bear; how fat quail sizzled when roasted. …

For days, Singing-owl had considered exile or suicide. But he knew the one would be spent in temptation to see loved ones again. And there was no honor in the other.

Now Smallpox was to be finally outwitted. Singing-owl was fasting once more. But this time the fasting would go on, until there was nothing left.

He smiled faintly and pulled the buffalo robe tighter around him. At least, he thought, the laughing has stopped.

2 **frantic** very excited – 4 **taunt** [ɔ:] remark made to hurt s.o.'s feelings – 10 **to clutch** to hold fast to – 14 **to huddle** *here:* to curl up (sich zusammenkauern) – 19 **willow hoop** Reifen aus Weidenzweig – 20 **scolding** words of criticism (*e.g.* blaming children for behaving badly) – 21 **quail** Wachtel – **to sizzle** to make a hissing sound – 22 **suicide** killing oneself – 23 **in temptation to do s.th.** wanting to do s.th. which is bad or not allowed

Biographical Notes

Russell Bates, born in 1941, is from Anadarko, Oklahoma. He belongs to the Kiowa writers, a group of younger authors of whom the Pulitzer Prize winner N. Scott Momaday (House Made of Dawn, *1968) is the most famous.*

Bates had been in the Air Force for four years when he was seriously injured in a duty accident. While in hospital he turned to writing (formerly a "neglected hobby") as a sort of therapy.

He then studied creative writing at the University of Oklahoma and has published a number of short stories and children's books. He has written extensively for television, for example, he is the author of a Star Trek *screenplay and has been a contributing screen writer for* Battlestar Galactica, *broadcast by ABC-TV.*

He lives alternately in Anadarko and Los Angeles. Bates is particularly interested in science fiction writings by and about American Indians.

Ordinary science fiction deals with all kinds of technical innovations in a distant future and tells the readers about problems future generations may have to cope with. "Rite of Encounter," however, has been given a strange twist. Instead of setting the story in the future the author evokes the past and describes a fantastic situation back in the 19th century: the symbolic meeting of a young Kiowa Indian and Black Smallpox, a figure personifying that deadly disease.

Simon J. Ortiz

Pennstuwehniyaahtsi: Quuti's Story

"Quuti told me this story," Santiago said to Cholly, his 12-year old grandson, as they walked from their sheep camp in the mountain canyon to the Pueblo. "I don't know how much of it is true but there are true things in it. He told it to me some years ago and it is about a time long before that, perhaps when I was a little boy.

"Quuti was already no longer a child when he was taken by some white people who were teachers of the belief of the Mericano. Quuti said, 'We had been told this would happen. My grandmother was in great fear of them. When they would come around, she would take us children up to the hills and wait until they left. But it was one day when we were not prepared that they came. Two of them in a buckboard and another on a horse.

"'They just simply took me. They had a piece of paper on which was written something that would take me. My grandmother and my father and mother protested but it was of no avail. They said our leaders had agreed; it was written in the paper. So I went. My family and I cried. My mother packed me something to eat, dried meat and bread, what little we had. My father gave me a cornmeal pouch which he told me to hide. The white people put me in the buckboard and off we went.

"'That evening we camped.We headed east but I didn't know then where we were although years later I did.

"'They built a fire and cooked something. I took my sack and started to eat my food but the woman grabbed it from me and threw it away. The coyotes probably ate it. I started to cry because I was afraid they meant to starve me; such things had happened to our people in captivity. I knew that from the stories told by elder people. The woman pulled me out of the buckboard and sat me down on the ground, and she gave me a bowl with mushy stuff, hard

2 **Pueblo** Indian village in the Southwest – 7 **Mericano** American – 11 **buckboard** light, four-wheeled carriage – 14 **of no avail** of no use, in vain – 17 **cornmeal** grain (of corn) ground to powder (a sacred and powerful gift, here symbolizing protection) – **pouch** small bag – 19 **to head** to go in a certain direction – 23 **to starve s.o.** not to give s.o. any food at all – 26 **mushy** soft (like boiled cornmeal)

bread, and meat. I started to eat then as I was glad they weren't going to starve me, but the woman grabbed my hand and put a metal thing in my fingers and stuck it into the meat. She was talking to me but at that time I didn't understand a word of it.

"'The woman then showed me by using her metal thing to put food into her mouth. I tried but I was clumsy at it, and I thought it would take me all night to eat my supper. I learned that I didn't have to eat my bread with the thing which I learned later was called a fork. I guess I started learning then how the Mericano lived their lives.

"'It is much simpler, of course, and easier to eat with the fingers but they preferred to make it difficult. It makes them feel better, maybe more intelligent, maybe more skillful, to live such complicated lives,' Quuti said.

"Quuti said things like that about the Mericano," Santiago said. "He said he learned so many unnecessary and pointless things at the place where he was taken to. But he went ahead and learned because it was required. 'I became a good Indian,' he would say and laugh.

"Let's stop for a while, Good Indian," Santiago said to Cholly, and they sat at the roadside on a large rock.

"Where did they take him, Grandfather?" Cholly wanted to know.

"Well, after camp that night, they went to a large town where he was put on the train with other Indian children. 'Some were just babies, little,' Quuti said. 'We were all sad as we looked out of the windows at the land flying away from us. Travelling for days and nights, we finally stopped and, later, after I learned some Mericano words I could name the place. Pennstuwehniyaahtsi. It was a school there and that was the place where we were to learn how it was to live like the Mericano.

"'And they taught us or tried to, and we tried also because we had no choice. If we didn't, we didn't get anything to eat, or we got locked up, or had to do hard extra work until our hands would bleed. Most of us learned how to speak in Mericano although it was hard to say the strange words. And to write it.

"'We could not speak our own languages because that was not allowed and because there was no one else who spoke similarly. We were all different peoples from each other. But we found ways, and we even learned to talk with each other in our own ways even if we would be punished when we got caught. Sometimes I would go to the barn and talk to the cows. They would just look at me, of course, but at least I could hear myself and I would not

6 **clumsy** without skill – 15 **to require** to ask, to order to do s.th. – 34 **peoples** *here:* Indian tribes

forget the sound of my own language. I surely must have told those cows a lot of stories.'"

Cholly and his grandfather walked the miles eastward toward the Pueblo, and there was no sound except the story, their footsteps, and the calls of crows once in a while.

"'I stayed at the school called Carlyle,'" Santiago said as Quuti had told them, "'for about three years. One day because I had learned I was fifteen years old, I decided that I had enough of the Mericano's teaching. I was already a man and I was still being treated as a child, and I was concerned that my parents needed my help. And I was worried – I thought about it a lot – that I was becoming more like the Mericano than one of our people.

"'So I told the person in charge of us, and he stared at me for a while and then said, William – that was my Mericano name – you are a good Indian boy and you're becoming a fine blacksmith. It is a good trade; the United States needs skilled workers like you for we are going to be the greatest nation in the world. And I knew that I was never going to go home if I stayed in that Mericano place. So I decided that night I would leave.

"'I told this Chisheh from San Carlos I was leaving. He was younger than me and he cried but he wished me a good journey. That night we packed me some food and a few clothes, and he taught me a song which meant this: Run, the wind speeds you. Walk, the trees hide you. Speak, the birds hear you. Sing, your voice comforts you. It was a song his people sang in their fight against the Mericano soldiers.'

"So Quuti left Pennstuwehniyaahtsi," Santiago said. "It must have been late autumn when he did because he got caught in a snow storm." Cholly noticed that the afternoon sun was nearing the horizon. They had walked for miles and Santiago had kept up the same rhythm, never seeming to strain, his arms and hands swinging and indicating points in Quuti's story.

"'I had walked for many days. A storm came suddenly, and I almost froze. Never had I seen anything like that. It felt like the wind was blowing me more steps backward than I took forward. Finally, I found a barn in which I took shelter. I had to pull ice from my hair. There were cows in that barn and they kept me from freezing. I think it was two days and nights that I stayed. The next morning the snow was as high as the door of the barn, and the wind was

5 **crow** [krəʊ] – 9 **to be concerned** to be worried – 14 **blacksmith** s.o. who makes and repairs things made of iron, especially horseshoes – **trade** a skilled job – 18 **Chisheh** another name for the Apaches – 27 **to strain** to make a great effort – 28 **to indicate** to point out – 32 **to take shelter** to protect oneself (from rain, cold, etc.)

still blowing and bitter cold. I was afraid of the cold, and I was afraid of getting caught and sent back to the school.

"'I didn't know what I should do, but finally I decided I would find the people who owned the barn and cows and tell them the truth. I would tell them I was only on my way back to my people in the west, and I hoped they would have compassion and not report me to authorities. I was very hungry. After many many days of walking, I had run out of food, and I had only the cows' milk for nourishment. And so I started to dig out of the barn.

"'I had managed to push the barn door open a little and had begun to dig for a while when I heard a sound, and I listened and it sounded like someone was digging too. And it was.

"'Suddenly, the snow fell open, and there was a man standing in front of me who was so startled he dropped his shovel. And then he said something, but I didn't understand. I thought the cold had frozen my ears and brain so I couldn't understand or I had so quickly forgotten the Mericano language. But I soon figured out it wasn't Mericano he was speaking; it was another language.

"'Anyway, I understood from his gestures that he had been digging a tunnel through the snow so he could get to the barn to see after his cows. He was worried about them and we went into the barn, and he was so glad to see they were alright he started to kiss them and hug them and rub their hides to warm them up. And talking to them in this strange language. And I knew he wasn't Mericano for I had never seen any of them act like this man.

"'He was smiling and laughing because he was so happy, and then he started to milk the cows whose teats were so full they must have been hurting. So I helped him. After we finished milking and fed the cows, he pulled me along to his house through the tunnel he had made in the snow. A wife and children were there and they all set to work in making me feel at home. I was still half frozen and I had on clothes that were worn and dirty.

"'The man put me into a tub of warm water and then I was fed. And all this time, they were talking to me but I couldn't understand them, and I said a few things in Mericano and they couldn't understand that either. So I said some things in our language too and it was all the same, and we got along just

6 **compassion** pity for s.o.'s sufferings – **authorities** those who rule and make laws – 8 **nourishment** [ʌ] food – 13 **startled** surprised – **shovel** [ʌ] s.th. to dig with – 16 **to figure out** to work out, to understand – 21 **to hug** to put one's arms around s.o. (to show love) – **hide** animal's skin – 25 **teats** [i:] where the cow's milk comes out – 33 **to get along (with s.o.)** to feel at ease with s.o.

fine. I was happy to be warm and not hungry and freezing anymore, and they were kind, friendly, and compassionate.

"'I tried to explain from where I had been coming and where I was going but it didn't seem to make any impression at all. After a couple of days as I got my strength back, I wanted to leave but I owed that family something for saving my life, and so I stayed for a few more days to help them out with their farm. I think by then the woman and man understood where I was headed and why, and they indicated they wanted to help but it seemed to them to be so far away where I was going and it was winter and fearfully cold.

"'Those people, they knew about journeys and difficulties, they got me to understand, and they asked me to stay until the winter was over. So I stayed until spring came. We never spoke any Mericano but I learned to speak their language a little, and they learned to speak a little of ours, especially the children, a boy and a girl. Their hair was so yellow it shone.

"'I have never forgotten them and their name. Yoonson. They were a fine and caring family. Yoonson. When I got married and my first son was born I called him that – Yoonson. That journey was hard but if it wasn't for those people I would have never made it home.'"

Cholly could see the smoke rising from chimneys in the Pueblo and he was glad for that. He was tired but Santiago still seemed to be walking strongly along. The wind was colder now and had started to pick up and the sun had dropped below the mountain ridge.

"So Quuti arrived home safely," Santiago said, "on that long journey, and I believe it is mostly true." Santiago smiled. "Quuti was a fine and good man."

When they arrived home and were warming themselves by the kitchen stove, Santiago, smiling again, said to Cholly's mother, "That son of yours is quite a walker. He nearly walked my poor legs off. I think he would have made old man, beloved Quuti, a good companion on his walk from Pennstuwehniyaahtsi."

7 **to be headed** to travel in a certain direction – 17 **if it wasn't for those people** without them – 21 **to pick up** to become stronger – 22 **mountain ridge** long row of mountains – 26 **stove** kind of oven used to heat a room – 28 **companion** [æ] s.o. to do things with, friend

Biographical Notes

Among contemporary Native American authors Simon J. Ortiz is one of the prominent voices, enjoying worldwide renown. He was born in Albuquerque in 1941 and grew up in the Acoma Pueblo community in New Mexico. After formal schooling by the BIA (Bureau of Indian Affairs) and within the state and Catholic education systems, he studied at several colleges including the Universities of New Mexico and Iowa. Ortiz has been a journalist, clerk, soldier, laborer, public relations director and last but not least an instructor in Native American literature and creative writing at various colleges.

He presently lives in Albuquerque, but travels extensively reading his works to people all over the world.

Ortiz, who is currently working on a full-length novel, has published poetry and short stories of outstanding literary quality. His anthology Going for the Rain *(1976), for example, is a collection of short informal poems written in a simple colloquial style. Combining the literary traditions of white and Native American writers, the author portrays his often bitter experience of everyday reality.*

"Pennstuwehniyaahtsi: Quuti's Story" has been taken from the collection of short stories, Fightin' *(1983). According to Gary Snyder, a famous beat poet, these stories are "little parables of daily failure, courage, and love" in the lives of ordinary people, both Indian and white.*

Leslie Marmon Silko

Lullaby

The sun had gone down but the snow in the wind gave off its own light. It came in thick tufts like new wool – washed before the weaver spins it. Ayah reached out for it like her own babies had, and she smiled when she remembered how she had laughed at them. She was an old woman now, and her life had become memories. She sat down with her back against the wide cottonwood tree, feeling the rough bark on her back bones; she faced east and listened to the wind and snow sing a high-pitched Yeibechei song. Out of the wind she felt warmer, and she could watch the wide fluffy snow fill in her tracks, steadily, until the direction she had come from was gone. By the light of the snow she could see the dark outline of the big arroyo a few feet away. She was sitting on the edge of Cebolleta Creek, where in the springtime the thin cows would graze on grass already chewed flat to the ground. In the wide deep creek bed where only a trickle of water flowed in the summer, the skinny cows would wander, looking for new grass along winding paths splashed with manure.

Ayah pulled the old army blanket over her head like a shawl. Jimmie's blanket – the one he had sent to her. That was a long time ago and the green wool was faded, and it was unraveling on the edges. She did not want to think about Jimmie. So she thought about the weaving and the way her mother had done it. On the tall wooden loom set into the sand under a tamarack tree for shade. She could see it clearly. She had been only a little girl when her grandma gave her the wooden combs to pull the twigs and burrs from the raw, freshly washed wool. And while she combed the wool,

lullaby ['lʌləbaɪ] a quiet song meant to help a child go to sleep – 2 **tuft** a cluster; s.th. that grows close together – 5 **cottonwood** amerikanische Pappelart – 7 **high-pitched** sung in a high voice and often shrill in tone – **Yeibechei** Navajo "Grandfather of the Gods"; Yeibechei songs are performed by teams of masked dancers, and in these songs the voices of the Gods are heard – 10 **arroyo** [ə'rɔɪəʊ] *(southwest U.S.)* a steep-sided watercourse, usually dry except after heavy rain – 13 **creek** *(A.E.)* a small stream – 15 **manure** [mə'njʊə] dung – 18 **to fade** to become pale in colour – **to unravel** [ʌn'rævəl] of s.th. woven or knitted: to become undone – 20 **loom** a frame that is used for weaving thread into cloth – 21 **tamarack** a North American larch tree (Lärchenart) – 22 **twig** a very small, thin branch – 23 **burr** fruit of some plants that has little hooks on the outside so that it sticks to clothes, etc. (Klette)

her grandma sat beside her, spinning a silvery strand of yarn around the smooth cedar spindle. Her mother worked at the loom with yarns dyed bright yellow and red and gold. She watched them dye the yarn in boiling black pots full of beeweed petals, juniper berries, and sage. The blankets her mother made were soft and woven so tight that rain rolled off them like birds' feathers. Ayah remembered sleeping warm on cold windy nights, wrapped in her mother's blankets on the hogan's sandy floor.

The snow drifted now, with the northwest wind hurling it in gusts. It drifted up around her black overshoes – old ones with little metal buckles. She smiled at the snow which was trying to cover her little by little. She could remember when they had no black rubber overshoes; only the high buckskin leggings that they wrapped over their elk-hide moccasins. If the snow was dry or frozen, a person could walk all day and not get wet, and in the evenings the beams of the ceiling would hang with lengths of pale buckskin leggings, drying out slowly.

She felt peaceful remembering. She didn't feel cold anymore. Jimmie's blanket seemed warmer than it had ever been. And she could remember the morning he was born. She could remember whispering to her mother who was sleeping on the other side of the hogan, to tell her it was time now. She did not want to wake the others. The second time she called to her, her mother stood up and pulled on her shoes; she knew. They walked to the old stone hogan together, Ayah walking a step behind her mother. She waited alone, learning the rhythms of the pains while her mother went to call the old woman to help them. The morning was already warm even before dawn and Ayah smelled the bee flowers blooming and the young willow growing at the springs. She could remember that so clearly, but his birth merged into the births of the other children and to her it became all the same birth. They named him for the summer morning and in English they called him Jimmie.

It wasn't like Jimmie died. He just never came back, and one day a dark

1 **yarn** thread made from wool or cotton, which is used for making cloth – 2 **smooth** [ð] not rough – **to dye s.th.** to colour s.th. by soaking it in colouring solution – 4 **beeweed** bee balm, a wildflower – **petal** ['petl] white or coloured leaf-like part of a flower – **juniper** ['dʒu:nɪpə] Wacholder – **sage** Salbei – 7 **hogan** ['həʊgən] the round earth-covered Navajo house; the door faces east to make sure the inhabitants live in harmony with nature – 8 **gust** short, strong, sudden rush of wind – 9 **buckle** a metal frame used to fasten a belt or strap – 11 **buckskin** soft leather made from the skin of deer – 12 **leggings** a leg covering made of leather – 14 **beam** wooden support visible on a ceiling – **ceiling** ['si:lɪŋ] the top part inside a room, opposite the floor – 25 **willow** a tree that usually grows near water (Weide) – 26 **to merge into** to become indistinguishable from – 29 **it wasn't like** it was not as if

blue sedan with white writing on its doors pulled up in front of the boxcar shack where the rancher let the Indians live. A man in a khaki uniform trimmed in gold gave them a yellow piece of paper and told them that Jimmie was dead. He said the army would try to get the body back and then it would be shipped to them; but it wasn't likely because the helicopter had burned after it crashed. All of this was told to Chato because he could understand English. She stood inside the doorway holding the baby while Chato listened. Chato spoke English like a white man and he spoke Spanish too. He was taller than the white man and he stood straighter too. Chato didn't explain why: he just told the military man they could keep the body if they found it. The white man looked bewildered; he nodded his head and he left. Then Chato looked at her and shook his head. "Goddamn," he said in English, and then he told her "Jimmie isn't coming home anymore," and when he spoke, he used the words to speak of the dead. She didn't cry then, but she hurt inside with anger. And she mourned him as the years passed, when a horse fell with Chato and broke his leg, and the white rancher told them he wouldn't pay Chato until he could work again. She mourned Jimmie because he would have worked for his father then; he would have saddled the big bay horse and ridden the fence lines each day, with wire cutters and heavy gloves, fixing the breaks in the barbed wire and putting the stray cattle back inside again.

She mourned him after the white doctors came to take Danny and Ella away. She was at the shack alone that day when they came. It was back in the days before they hired Navajo women to go with them as interpreters. She recognized one of the doctors. She had seen him at the children's clinic at Cañoncito about a month ago. They were wearing khaki uniforms and they waved papers at her and a black ball-point pen, trying to make her understand their English words. She was frightened by the way they looked at the children, like the lizard watches the fly. Danny was swinging on the tire swing in the elm tree behind the rancher's house, and Ella was toddling

1 **sedan** [sə'dæn] *(A.E.)* a closed automobile having a front and rear seat – **boxcar** *(A.E.)* a railway wagon in which goods are transported – 2 **shack** a small, poorly built hut – 6 **Chato** Ayah's husband – 11 **bewildered** completely confused and not knowing what to do next – 15 **to mourn s.o.** to be very sad because s.o. has died and to show this in the way one behaves – 18 **bay** reddish-brown (used to describe the colour of a horse) – 20 **barbed wire** strong wire with sharp points sticking out of it – **stray** (of a domestic animal) having wandered away from home – 27 **ball-point pen** biro – 29 **lizard** Eidechse – **tire swing** an automobile tyre (*A.E.* spelling: tire) suspended from a branch, on which one may ride back and forth

around the front door, dragging the broomstick horse Chato made for her. Ayah could see they wanted her to sign the papers, and Chato had taught her to sign her name. It was something she was proud of. She only wanted them to go, and to take their eyes away from her children.

She took the pen from the man without looking at his face and she signed the papers in three different places he pointed to. She stared at the ground by their feet and waited for them to leave. But they stood there and began to point and gesture at the children. Danny stopped swinging. Ayah could see his face. She moved suddenly and grabbed Ella into her arms; the child squirmed, trying to get back to her toys. Ayah ran with the baby toward Danny; she screamed for him to run and then she grabbed him around his chest and carried him too. She ran south into the foothills of juniper trees and black lava rock. Behind her she heard the doctors running, but they had been taken by surprise, and as the hills became steeper and the cholla cactus were thicker, they stopped. When she reached the top of the hill, she stopped too to listen in case they were circling around her. But in a few minutes she heard a car engine start and they drove away. The children had been too surprised to cry while she ran with them. Danny was shaking and Ella's little fingers were gripping Ayah's blouse.

She stayed up in the hills for the rest of the day, sitting on a black lava boulder in the sunshine where she could see for miles all around her. The sky was light blue and cloudless, and it was warm for late April. The sun warmth relaxed her and took the fear and anger away. She lay back on the rock and watched the sky. It seemed to her that she could walk into the sky, stepping through clouds endlessly. Danny played with little pebbles and stones, pretending they were birds, eggs and then little rabbits. Ella sat at her feet and dropped fistfuls of dirt into the breeze, watching the dust and particles of sand intently. Ayah watched a hawk soar high above them, dark wings gliding; hunting or only watching, she did not know. The hawk was patient and he circled all afternoon before he disappeared around the high volcanic peak the Mexicans call Guadalupe.

Late in the afternoon, Ayah looked down at the gray boxcar shack with the paint all peeled from the wood; the stovepipe on the roof was rusted and

10 **to squirm** to move one's body from side to side because one is nervous or uncomfortable – 14 **to take s.o. by surprise** to act suddenly when the other person is not ready or does not expect it – **cholla** tree-like cactus of the southwestern U.S. – 21 **boulder** a large rock – 25 **pebble** a smooth, rounded stone – 27 **breeze** light wind – 28 **hawk** a bird of prey (Habicht) – **to soar** to rise quickly (into the air, the sky) – 33 **to peel** (of paint, skin, etc.) to come off – **stove** type of oven that provides heat

crooked. The fire she had built that morning in the oil-drum stove had burned out. Ella was asleep in her lap now and Danny sat close to her, complaining that he was hungry; he asked when they would go to the house. "We will stay up here until your father comes," she told him, "because those white men were chasing us." The boy remembered then and he nodded at her silently.

If Jimmie had been there he could have read those papers and explained to her what they said. Ayah would have known, then, never to sign them. The doctors came back the next day and they brought a BIA policeman with them. They told Chato they had her signature and that was all they needed. Except for the kids. She listened to Chato sullenly; she hated him when he told her it was the old woman who died in the winter, spitting blood; it was her old grandma who had given the children this disease. "They don't spit blood," she said coldly. "The whites lie." She held Ella and Danny close to her, ready to run to the hills again. "I want a medicine man first," she said to Chato, not looking at him. He shook his head. "It's too late now. The policeman is with them. You signed the paper." His voice was gentle.

It was worse than if they had died; to lose the children and to know that somewhere, in a place called Colorado, in a place full of sick and dying strangers, her children were without her. There had been babies that died soon after they were born, and one that died before he could walk. She had carried them herself, up to the boulders and great pieces of the cliff that long ago crashed down from Long Mesa; she laid them in the crevices of sandstone and buried them in fine brown sand with round quartz pebbles that washed down from the hills in the rain. She had endured it because they had been with her. But she could not bear this pain. She did not sleep for a long time after they took her children. She stayed on the hill where they had fled the first time, and she slept rolled up in the blanket Jimmie had sent her. She carried the pain in her belly and it was fed by everything she saw; the blue sky of their last day together and the dust and pebbles they played with; the swing in the elm tree and broomstick horse choked life from her. The pain filled her stomach and there was no room for food or for her lungs to fill with air. The air and the food would have been theirs.

1 **crooked** ['krʊkɪd] not straight – **drum** a barrel – **oil-drum stove** stove made out of an old oil barrel – 9 **BIA** Bureau of Indian Affairs, a division of the U.S. Department of the Interior that administers federal programmes for Native Americans living on reservations – 13 **this disease** tuberculosis – 23 **mesa** ['meɪsə] (from the Spanish word for *table*) flat-topped mountain, common in the southwestern U.S. – **crevice** ['krevɪs] crack or gap in rock or between large boulders – 25 **to endure s.th.** to bear s.th. patiently – 31 **to choke** to make breathing impossible

She hated Chato, not because he let the policeman and doctors put the screaming children in the government car, but because he had taught her to sign her name. Because it was like the old ones always told her about learning their language or any of their ways; it endangered you. She slept alone on the hill until the middle of November when the first snows came. Then she made a bed for herself where the children had slept. She did not lie down beside Chato again until many years later, when he was sick and shivering and only her body could keep him warm. The illness came after the white rancher told Chato he was too old to work for him any more, and Chato and his old woman should be out of the shack by the next afternoon because the rancher had hired new people to work there. That had satisfied her. To see how the white man repaid Chato's years of loyalty and work. All of Chato's fine-sounding English talk didn't change things.

It snowed steadily and the luminous light from the snow gradually diminished into the darkness. Somewhere in Cebolleta a dog barked and other village dogs joined with it. Ayah looked in the direction she had come, from the bar where Chato was buying the wine. Sometimes he told her to go on ahead and wait; and then he never came. And when she finally went back looking for him, she would find him passed out at the bottom of the wooden steps to Azzie's Bar. All the wine would be gone and most of the money too, from the pale blue check that came to them once a month in a government envelope. It was then that she would look at his face and his hands, scarred by ropes and the barbed wire of all those years, and she would think "this man is a stranger;" for 40 years she had smiled at him and cooked his food, but he remained a stranger. She stood up again, with the snow almost to her knees, and she walked back to find Chato.

It was hard to walk in the deep snow and she felt the air burn in her lungs. She stopped a short distance from the bar to rest and readjust the blanket. But this time he wasn't waiting for her on the bottom step with his old Stetson hat pulled down and his shoulders hunched up in his long wool overcoat.

She was careful not to slip on the wooden steps. When she pushed the door open, warm air and cigarette smoke hit her face. She looked around slowly and deliberately, in every corner, in every dark place that the old man might find to sleep. The bar-owner didn't like Indians in there, especially Navajos, but he let Chato come in because he could talk Spanish like he was one of them. The men at the bar stared at her, and the bartender saw that she

19 **to pass out** to faint, to lose consciousness – 34 **deliberately** *here:* slowly and carefully

left the door open wide. Snowflakes were flying inside like moths and melting into a puddle on the oiled wood floor. He motioned at her to close the door, but she did not see him. She held herself straight and walked across the room slowly, searching the room with every step. The snow in her hair melted and she could feel it on her forehead. At the far corner of the room, she saw red flames at the mica window of the old stove door; she looked behind the stove just to make sure. The bar got quiet except for the Spanish polka music playing on the jukebox. She stood by the stove and shook the snow from her blanket and held it near the stove to dry. The wet wool smell reminded her of new-born goats in early March, brought inside to warm near the fire. She felt calm.

In past years they would have told her to get out. But her hair was white now and her face was wrinkled. They looked at her like she was a spider crawling slowly across the room. They were afraid; she could feel the fear. She looked at their faces steadily. They reminded her of the first time the white people brought her children back to her that winter. Danny had been shy and hid behind the thin white woman who brought them. And the baby had not known her until Ayah took her into her arms, and then Ella had nuzzled close to her as she had when she was nursing. The blonde woman was nervous and kept looking at a dainty gold watch on her wrist. She sat on the bench near the small window and watched the dark snow clouds gather around the mountains; she was worrying about the unpaved road. She was frightened by what she saw inside too; the strips of venison drying on a rope across the ceiling and the children jabbering excitedly in a language she did not know. So they stayed for only a few hours. Ayah watched the government car disappear down the road and she knew they were already being weaned from these lava hills and from this sky. The last time they came was in early June, and Ella stared at her the way the men in the bar were now staring. Ayah did not try to pick her up; she smiled at her instead and spoke cheerfully to Danny. When he tried to answer her, he could not seem to remember and he spoke English words with the Navajo. But he gave her a scrap of paper that he had found somewhere and carried in his pocket; it was folded

1 **moth** an insect with large wings, which usually flies about at night – 6 **mica** ['maɪkə] (made of) a hard mineral that has great resistance to heat – 13 **wrinkled** ['rɪŋkld] having many lines in the skin – **spider** Spinne – 19 **to nuzzle s.o.** to gently move one's nose and mouth against s.o. – **to nurse** *here:* to feed by sucking milk from the mother's breast – 20 **dainty** small and pretty – 23 **venison** ['venɪzn] meat of deer or other wild animals – 26 **to wean s.o. from s.th.** to gradually make s.o. stop doing or being used to s.th. (entwöhnen)

in half, and he shyly looked up at her and said it was a bird. She asked Chato if they were home for good this time. He spoke to the white woman and she shook her head. "How much longer," he asked, and she said she didn't know; but Chato saw how she stared at the boxcar shack. Ayah turned away then. She did not say good-bye.

She felt satisfied that the men in the bar feared her. Maybe it was her face and the way she held her mouth with teeth clenched tight, like there was nothing anyone could do to her now. She walked north down the road, searching for the old man. She did this because she had the blanket, and there would be no place for him except with her and the blanket in the old adobe barn near the arroyo. They always slept there when they came to Cebolleta. If the money and the wine were gone, she would be relieved because then they could go home again; back to the old hogan with a dirt roof and rock walls where she herself had been born. And the next day the old man could go back to the few sheep they still had, to follow along behind them, guiding them into dry sandy arroyos where sparse grass grew. She knew he did not like walking behind old ewes when for so many years he rode big quarter horses and worked with cattle. But she wasn't sorry for him; he should have known all along what would happen.

There had not been enough rain for their garden in five years; and that was when Chato finally hitched a ride into the town and brought back brown boxes of rice and sugar and big tin cans of welfare peaches. After that, at the first of the month they went to Cebolleta to ask the postmaster for the check; and then Chato would go to the bar and cash it. They did this as they planted the garden every May, not because anything would survive the summer dust, but because it was time to do this. And the journey passed the days that smelled silent and dry like the caves above the canyon with yellow painted buffaloes on their walls.

He was walking along the pavement when she found him. He did not stop or turn around when he heard her behind him. She walked beside him and she noticed how slowly he moved now. He smelled strong of woodsmoke and urine. Lately he had been forgetting. Sometimes he called her by his sister's name and she had been gone for a long time. Once she had found him

7 **clenched** pressed together – 11 **adobe** [ə'dəʊbɪ] (made of) unburnt sun-dried brick – 16 **sparse** ['spɑ:s] opposite of dense – 17 **ewe** [ju:] female sheep – 18 **quarter horse** a breed of strong horses developed in the western U.S. – 21 **to hitch a ride** to hitchhike – 22 **welfare** *here:* subsidized by the government

wandering on the road to the white man's ranch, and she asked him why he was going that way; he laughed at her and said "You know they can't run that ranch without me," and he walked on determined, limping on the leg that had been crushed many years before. Now he looked at her curiously, as if for the first time, but he kept shuffling along, moving slowly along the side of the highway. His gray hair had grown long and spread out on the shoulders of the long overcoat. He wore the old felt hat pulled down over his ears. His boots were worn out at the toes and he had stuffed pieces of an old red shirt in the holes. The rags made his feet look like little animals up to their ears in snow. She laughed at his feet; the snow muffled the sound of her laugh. He stopped and looked at her again. The wind had quit blowing and the snow was falling straight down; the southeast sky was beginning to clear and Ayah could see a star.

"Let's rest awhile," she said to him. They walked away from the road and up the slope to the giant boulders that had tumbled down from the red sandrock mesa throughout the centuries of rainstorms and earth tremors. In a place where the boulders shut out the wind, they sat down with their backs against the rock. She offered half of the blanket to him and they sat wrapped together.

The storm passed swiftly. The clouds moved east. They were massive and full, crowding together across the sky. She watched them with the feeling of horses – steely blue-gray horses startled across the sky. The powerful haunches pushed into the distances and the tail hairs streamed white mist behind them. The sky cleared. Ayah saw that there was nothing between her and the stars. The light was crystalline. There was no shimmer, no distortion through earth haze. She breathed the clarity of the night sky; she smelled the purity of the half moon and the stars. He was lying on his side with his knees pulled up near his belly for warmth. His eyes were closed now, and in the light from the stars and the moon, he looked young again.

She could see it descend out of the night sky; an icy stillness from the edge of the thin moon. She recognized the freezing. It came gradually, sinking snowflake by snowflake until the crust was heavy and deep. It had the strength of the stars in Orion, and its journey was endless. Ayah knew that with the wine he would sleep. He would not feel it. She tucked the blanket

3 **to limp** to walk in an uneven way because one leg is hurt – 5 **to shuffle** to walk without lifting one's feet off the ground properly – 10 **to muffle** to deaden a sound, to make a sound less loud – 11 **to quit** to stop – 15 **slope** a stretch of ground rising at one end – 16 **tremor** a light earthquake – 22 **to startle** *here:* to move quickly as if frightened – 23 **haunch** the fleshly part of the body around the hip – 26 **haze** thin mist (Dunst)

around him, remembering how it was when Ella had been with her; and she felt the rush so big inside her heart for the babies. And she sang the only song she knew to sing for babies. She could not remember if she had ever sung it to her children, but she knew that her grandmother had sung it and her mother had sung it:

The earth is your mother,
she holds you.
The sky is your father,
he protects you.
Sleep,
sleep,
Rainbow is your sister,
she loves you.
The winds are your brothers,
they sing to you.
Sleep,
sleep,
We are together always
We are together always
There never was a time
when this
was not so.

Biographical Notes

Leslie Marmon Silko was born in 1948 and grew up on the Laguna Pueblo reservation near Albuquerque, New Mexico. Her great-grandfather, a white surveyor and trader, had come to Laguna in 1872. This is what she says about her ancestry: "We (= my family) are mixed bloods – Laguna, Mexican, white ... All those languages, all those ways of living are combined, and we live somewhere on the fringes of all three. But I don't apologize for this any more – not to whites, not to full bloods – our origin is unlike any other. My poetry, my storytelling rise out of this source." (Kenneth Rosen, Voices of the Rainbow, *p. 230, New York, 1975)*

Silko's creative impetus and sensibility apparently stem from this origin, a fact which becomes evident in her literary portrayal of alienated Native Americans torn between two cultures and trying to find themselves.

This identity crisis is most obvious in her famous novel Ceremony *(1977), which tells the story of Tayo, a young halfbreed from Laguna, who returns to the reservation after fighting against the Japanese in World War II. Being completely estranged from the old way of living as a result of the war and his battle fatigue, Tayo is restored to health by a medicine man whose "ceremony" proves the vitality of traditional Indian culture and its system of values.*

Leslie Silko has a B.A. in English from the University of New Mexico where she taught creative writing and Native American literature after graduation. She is now a well-known author (she received one of the MacArthur Foundation awards in 1981); apart from Ceremony *she has published poems and short stories (*Laguna Woman, *1974;* Storyteller, *1981) and many articles. Currently she lives in Tucson, Arizona, working on a second novel.*

Louise Erdrich

Snares

It began after church with Margaret and her small granddaughter, Lulu, and was not to end until the long days of Lent and a hard-packed snow. There were factions on the reservation, a treaty settlement in the Agent's hands. There were Chippewa who signed their names in the year 1924, and there were Chippewa who saw the cash offered as a flimsy bait. I was one and Fleur Pillager, Lulu's mother, was another who would not lift her hand to sign. It was said that all the power to witch, harm, or cure lay in Fleur, the lone survivor of the old Pillager clan. But as much as people feared Fleur, they listened to Margaret Kashpaw. She was the ringleader of the holdouts, a fierce, one-minded widow with a vinegar tongue.

Margaret Kashpaw had knots of muscles in her arms. Her braids were thin, gray as iron, and usually tied strictly behind her back so they wouldn't swing. She was plump as a basket below and tough as roots on top. Her face was gnarled around a beautiful sharp nose. Two shell earrings caught the light and flashed whenever she turned her head. She had become increasingly religious in the years after her loss, and finally succeeded in dragging me to the Benediction Mass, where I was greeted by Father Damien, from whom I occasionally won small sums at dice.

"Grandfather Nanapush," he smiled, "at last."

snare a trap for catching small animals, usually consisting of a loop (Schlinge) of rope or wire; anything used to trap s.o. or s.th. – 2 **Lent** the period of forty days before Easter – 3 **faction** a group within a larger group, which holds certain ideas – **the Agent** the Indian agent, an official representing the U.S. government in dealing with an Indian tribe – 4 **Chippewa** a group of tribes living on different reservations from Michigan to North Dakota – 5 **flimsy** weak, not very good – **bait** small amount of food put on a hook or in a trap in order to attract and catch a fish or animal – 7 **to witch** to harm by using supernatural powers – 8 **lone** *here:* only – 9 **ringleader** leader of a group of people who cause trouble – **holdout** person who resists an enemy and refuses to surrender – 10 **one-minded** single-minded, determined to achieve one's aim – **widow** woman whose husband has died – **vinegar** a sharp-tasting liquid made from sour wine; *here:* sharp – 11 **braid** *(A.E.; B.E.: plait)* a length of hair which has been twisted together and tied – 14 **gnarled** ['nɑ:ld] having rough skin that looks swollen and knotty – 17 **benediction** Segnung

"These benches are a hardship for an old man," I complained. "If you spread them with soft pine-needle cushions I'd have come before."

Father Damien stared thoughtfully at the rough pews, folded his hands inside the sleeves of his robe.

"You must think of their unyielding surfaces as helpful," he offered. "God sometimes enters the soul through the humblest parts of our anatomies, if they are sensitized to suffering."

"A god who enters through the rear door," I countered, "is no better than a thief."

Father Damien was used to me, and smiled as he walked to the altar. I adjusted my old bones, longing for some relief, trying not to rustle for fear of Margaret's jabbing elbow. The time was long. Lulu probed all my pockets with her fingers until she found a piece of hard candy. I felt no great presence in this cold place and decided, as my back end ached and my shoulders stiffened, that our original gods were better, the Chippewa characters who were not exactly perfect but at least did not require sitting on hard boards.

When Mass was over and the smell of incense was thick in all our clothes, Margaret, Lulu, and I went out into the starry cold, the snow and stubble fields, and began the long walk to our homes. It was dusk. On either side of us the heavy trees stood motionless and blue. Our footsteps squeaked against the dry snow, the only sound to hear. We spoke very little, and even Lulu ceased her singing when the moon rose to half, poised like a balanced cup. We knew the very moment someone else stepped upon the road.

We had turned a bend and the footfalls came unevenly, just out of sight. There were two men, one mixed-blood or white, from the drop of his hard boot soles, and the other one quiet, an Indian. Not long and I heard them talking close behind us. From the rough, quick tension of the Indian's language, I recognized Lazarre. And the mixed-blood must be Clarence Morrissey. The two had signed the treaty and spoke in its favor to anyone they could

2 **cushion** ['kʊʃn] s.th. filled with soft material to make a seat more comfortable – 3 **pew** [pju:] a long, wooden seat in a church – 5 **unyielding** not giving way, hard – 6 **humble** modest; low in status, not important – 8 **to counter** to say s.th. in reply, contradicting the previous statement – 11 **to rustle** ['rʌsl] to make a soft sound (as of leaves being moved by a breeze) – 12 **to jab** to push s.th. sharp into s.th. else – 14 **to ache** [eɪk] to hurt, to feel a steady pain – 17 **incense** ['--] substance that is burned for its sweet smell (Weihrauch) – 18 **stubble** the short stalks which are left standing in the fields after the corn has been harvested – 19 **dusk** the time just before night – 22 **to cease** [si:s] to stop – **poised** suspended in the air – 25 **from the drop of ...** I could tell this from the way he walked

collar at the store. They even came to people's houses to beg and argue that this was our one chance, our good chance, that the government would withdraw the offer. But wherever Margaret was, she slapped down their words like mosquitoes and said the only thing that lasts life to life is land. Money burns like tinder, flows like water. And as for promises, the wind is steadier. It is no wonder that, because she spoke so well, Lazarre and Clarence Morrissey wished to silence her. I sensed their bad intent as they passed us, an unpleasant edge of excitement in their looks and greetings.

They went on, disappeared in the dark brush.

"Margaret," I said, "we are going to cut back." My house was close, but Margaret kept walking forward as if she hadn't heard.

I took her arm, caught the little girl close, and started to turn us, but Margaret would have none of this and called me a coward. She grabbed the girl to her. Lulu, who did not mind getting tossed between us, laughed, tucked her hand into her grandma's pocket, and never missed a step. Two years ago she had tired of being carried, got up, walked. She had the balance of a little mink. She was slippery and clever, too, which was good because when the men jumped from the darkest area of brush and grappled with us half a mile on, Lulu slipped free and scrambled into the trees.

They were occupied with Margaret and me, at any rate. We were old enough to snap in two, our limbs dry as dead branches, but we fought as though our enemies were the Nadouissioux kidnappers of our childhood. Margaret uttered a war cry that had not been heard for fifty years, and bit Lazarre's hand to the bone, giving a wound which would later prove the death of him. As for Clarence, he had all he could do to wrestle me to the ground and knock me half unconscious. When he'd accomplished that, he tied me and tossed me into a wheelbarrow, which was hidden near the road for the purpose of lugging us to the Morrissey barn.

I came to my senses trussed to a manger, sitting on a bale. Margaret was roped to another bale across from me, staring straight forward in a rage, a line of froth caught between her lips. On either side of her, shaggy cows

1 **to collar s.o.** to catch people in order to speak to them – 3 **to withdraw s.th.** to take s.th. back – 5 **tinder** small pieces of dry wood and grass that burn easily – 7 **intent** intention – 13 **coward** s.o. who is easily frightened – 17 **mink** a small weasel-like animal (Nerz) – 18 **to grapple with s.o.** to struggle, to fight hard with s.o. – 21 **limb** [lɪm] an arm or a leg – 22 **Nadouissioux** name given to the Sioux by the Chippewa, their deadly enemies – 25 **to wrestle** ['resl] to fight with s.o. by forcing them to the ground – 29 **trussed** tied up very tightly with ropes – **manger** ['meɪndʒə] feeding box in a barn – 31 **froth** foam

chewed and shifted their thumping hooves. I rose and staggered, the weight of the manger on my back. I planned on Margaret biting through my ropes with her strong teeth, but then the two men entered.

I'm a talker, a fast-mouth who can't keep his thoughts straight, but lets fly with words and marvels at what he hears from his own mouth. I'm a smart one. I always was a devil for convincing women. And I wasn't too bad a shot, in other ways, at convincing men. But I had never been tied up before.

"Booshoo," I said. "Children, let us loose, your game is too rough!"

They stood between us, puffed with their secrets.

"Empty old windbag," said Clarence.

"I have a bargain for you," I said, looking for an opening. "Let us go and we won't tell Pukwan." Edgar Pukwan was the tribal police. "Boys get drunk sometimes and don't know what they're doing."

Lazarre laughed once, hard and loud. "We're not drunk," he said. "Just wanting what's coming to us, some justice, money out of it."

"Kill us," said Margaret. "We won't sign."

"Wait," I said. "My cousin Pukwan will find you boys, and have no mercy. Let us go. I'll sign and get it over with, and I'll persuade the old widow."

I signaled Margaret to keep her mouth shut. She blew air into her cheeks. Clarence looked expectantly at Lazarre, as if the show were over, but Lazarre folded his arms and was convinced of nothing.

"You lie when it suits, skinny old dog," he said, wiping at his lips as if in hunger. "It's her we want, anyway. We'll shame her so she shuts her mouth."

"Easy enough," I said, smooth, "now that you've got her tied. She's plump and good-looking. Eyes like a doe! But you forget that we're together, almost man and wife."

This wasn't true at all, and Margaret's face went rigid with tumbling fury and confusion. I kept talking.

"So of course if you do what you're thinking of doing you'll have to kill me afterward, and that will make my cousin Pukwan twice as angry, since I owe him a fat payment for a gun which he lent me and I never returned. All the same," I went on – their heads were spinning – "I'll forget you bad boys ever considered such a crime, something so terrible that Father Damien would nail you on boards just like in the example on the wall in church."

1 **to stagger** to walk unsteadily and with difficulty – 5 **to marvel** to be filled with surprise – 6 **to be a devil for doing s.th.** *(coll.)* to be very good at doing s.th. – **to convince** *here:* to persuade – 11 **bargain** an agreement between two people stating what each will do, pay or receive – 24 **smooth** [ð] *here:* in a steady voice – 25 **doe** [dəʊ] a female deer – 27 **rigid** stiff

"Quit jabbering." Lazarre stopped me in a deadly voice.

It was throwing pebbles in a dry lake. My words left no ripple. I saw in his eyes that he intended us great harm. I saw his greed. It was like watching an ugly design of bruises come clear for a moment and reconstructing the evil blows that made them.

I played my last card.

"Whatever you do to Margaret you are doing to the Pillager woman!" I dropped my voice. "The witch, Fleur Pillager, is her own son's wife."

Clarence was too young to be frightened, but his mouth hung in interested puzzlement. My words had a different effect on Lazarre, as a sudden light shone, a consequence he hadn't considered.

I cried out, seeing this, "Don't you know she can think about you hard enough to stop your heart?" Lazarre was still deciding. He raised his fist and swung it casually and tapped my face. It was worse not to be hit full on.

"Come near!" crooned Margaret in the old language. "Let me teach you how to die."

But she was trapped like a fox. Her earrings glinted and spun as she hissed her death song over and over, which signaled something to Lazarre, for he shook himself angrily and drew a razor from his jacket. He stropped it with fast, vicious movements while Margaret sang shriller, so full of hate that the ropes should have burned, shriveled, fallen from her body. My struggle set the manger cracking against the barn walls and further confused the cows, who bumped each other and complained. At a sign from Lazarre, Clarence sighed, rose, and smashed me. The last I saw before I blacked out, through the tiny closing pinhole of light, was Lazarre approaching Margaret with the blade.

When I woke, minutes later, it was to worse shock. For Lazarre had sliced Margaret's long braids off and was now, carefully, shaving her scalp. He started almost tenderly at the wide part, and then pulled the edge down each side of her skull. He did a clean job. He shed not one drop of her blood.

1 **to quit** to stop – 2 **pebble** a smooth, round stone – **ripple** a little wave on the surface of water; *here:* effect – 3 **greed** the desire to have more of s.th. (e.g. money, power) – 4 **bruise** [bru:z] mark on the skin left after you have hit s.o. – 5 **blow** [bləʊ] a hard hit that you give s.o. with your fist or with a weapon – 10 **puzzlement** confusion – 14 **casually** carelessly; without much interest – 15 **to croon** to speak in a sweet, gentle voice – 17 **to hiss** to make a sound like a long 's' – 19 **razor** ['reɪzə] knifelike instrument used for removing hair from skin – **to strop** to sharpen a razor on a piece of leather – 21 **to shrivel** to become dry and wrinkled like a plant without water – 29 **tenderly** gently, lovingly – 30 **to shed (shed, shed) blood** Blut vergießen

And I could not even speak to curse them. For pressing my jaw down, thick above my tongue, her braids, never cut in this life till now, were tied to silence me. Powerless, I tasted their flat, animal perfume.

It wasn't much later, or else it was forever, that we walked out into the night again. Speechless, we made our way in fierce pain down the road. I was damaged in spirit, more so than Margaret. For now she tucked her shawl over her naked head and forgot her own bad treatment. She called out in dread each foot of the way, for Lulu. But the smart, bold girl had hidden till all was clear and then run to Margaret's house. We opened the door and found her sitting by the stove in a litter of scorched matches and kindling. She had not the skill to start a fire, but she was dry-eyed. Though very cold, she was alert and then captured with wonder when Margaret slipped off her shawl.

"Where is your hair?" she asked.

I took my hand from my pocket. "Here's what's left of it. I grabbed this when they cut me loose." I was shamed by how pitiful I had been, relieved when Margaret snatched the thin gray braids from me and coiled them round her fist.

"I knew you would save them, clever man!" There was satisfaction in her voice.

I set the fire blazing. It was strange how generous this woman was to me, never blaming me or mentioning my failure. Margaret stowed her braids inside a birchbark box and merely instructed me to lay it in her grave, when that time occurred. Then she came near the stove with a broken mirror from beside her washstand and looked at her own image.

"My," she pondered, "my." She put the mirror down. "I'll take a knife to them."

And I was thinking too. I was thinking I would have to kill them.

But how does an aching and half-starved grandfather attack a young, well-fed Morrissey and a tall, sly Lazarre? Later, I rolled up in blankets in the corner by Margaret's stove, and I put my mind to this question throughout

1 **to curse s.o.** to swear at s.o., to say insulting things to s.o. – **jaw** bone into which one's teeth are set – 8 **dread** [e] fear – 10 **stove** type of oven for heating a room – **scorched** half-burned – **kindling** [ɪ] very dry pieces of wood used to light a fire – 12 **alert** fully attentive, wide awake – **to capture** [ˈkæptʃə] to take prisoner – 17 **to coil** to curve into a series of loops (wickeln) – 21 **generous** offering more than is expected or asked for – 23 **bark** outer covering of a tree – **birch** a tree with white bark – 24 **to occur** to happen, to come to pass – 26 **to ponder** to think about s.th. carefully – 29 **to starve** to suffer from lack of food – 30 **sly** clever at tricking people

that night until, exhausted, I slept. And I thought of it first thing next morning, too, and still nothing came. It was only after we had some hot *gaulette* and walked Lulu back to her mother that an idea began to grow.

Fleur let us in, hugged Lulu into her arms, and looked at Margaret, who took off her scarf and stood bald, face burning again with smoldered fire. She told Fleur all of what happened, sparing no detail. The two women's eyes held, but Fleur said nothing. She put Lulu down, smoothed the front of her calico shirt, flipped her heavy braids over her shoulders, tapped one finger on her perfect lips. And then, calm, she went to the washstand and scraped the edge of her hunting knife keen as glass. Margaret and Lulu and I watched as Fleur cut her braids off, shaved her own head, and folded the hair into a quilled skin pouch. Then she went out, hunting, and didn't bother to wait for night to cover her tracks.

I would have to go out hunting too.

I had no gun, but anyway that was a white man's revenge. I knew how to wound with barbs of words, but had never wielded a skinning knife against a human, much less two young men. Whomever I missed would kill me, and I did not want to die by their lowly hands.

In fact, I didn't think that after Margaret's interesting kindness I wanted to leave this life at all. Her head, smooth as an egg, was ridged delicately with bone, and gleamed as if it had been buffed with a flannel cloth. Maybe it was the strangeness that attracted me. She looked forbidding, but the absence of hair also set off her eyes, so black and full of lights. She reminded me of that queen from England, of a water snake or a shrewd young bird. The earrings, which seemed part of her, mirrored her moods like water, and when they were still rounds of green lights against her throat I seemed, again, to taste her smooth, smoky braids in my mouth.

I had better things to do than fight. So I decided to accomplish revenge as quickly as possible. I was a talker who used my brains as my weapon. When I hunted, I preferred to let my game catch itself.

3 **gaulette** (from French *galette*) bread shaped like a pancake – 5 **bald** [bɔːld] without hair on the top of the head – **to smolder** *(A.E. spelling; B.E.: smoulder)* to burn slowly without any flames – 6 **to spare** to leave out – 8 **calico** (made from) cotton cloth printed with bright designs – 10 **keen** *here:* sharp – 12 **quilled** ornamented with feathers – **pouch** a small bag – 16 **barb** a sharp curved point, e.g. on a fish-hook (Widerhaken) – **to wield** *here:* to use – 18 **lowly** low in rank or status, unworthy – 20 **ridged** with raised lines on its surface – 21 **to gleam** to reflect light, to shine with a soft light – **to buff** to polish – 22 **forbidding** unfriendly and threatening – 23 **to set s.th. off** to provide a contrast for s.th. thus making it look more attractive – 24 **shrewd** [ʃruːd] very clever – 30 **game** wild animals that are hunted for meat

Snares demand clever fingers and a scheming mind, and snares had never failed me. Snares are quiet, and best of all snares are slow. I wanted to give Lazarre and Morrissey time to consider why they had to strangle. I thought hard. One- or two-foot deadfalls are required beneath a snare so that a man can't put his hand up and loosen the knot. The snares I had in mind also required something stronger than a cord, which could be broken, and finer than a rope, which even Lazarre might see and avoid. I pondered this closely, yet even so I might never have found the solution had I not gone to Mass with Margaret and grown curious about the workings of Father Damien's pride and joy, the piano in the back of the church, the instrument whose keys he breathed on, polished, then played after services, and sometimes alone. I had noticed that his hands usually stayed near the middle of the keyboard, so I took the wires from either end.

In the meantime, I was not the only one concerned with punishing Lazarre and Clarence Morrissey. Fleur was seen in town. Her thick skirts brushed the snow into clouds behind her. Though it was cold she left her head bare so everyone could see the frigid sun glare off her skull. The light reflected in the eyes of Lazarre and Clarence, who were standing at the door of the pool hall. They dropped their cue sticks in the slush and ran back to Morrissey land. Fleur walked the four streets, once in each direction, then followed.

The two men told of her visit, how she passed through the Morrissey house touching here, touching there, sprinkling powders that ignited and stank on the hot stove. How Clarence swayed on his feet, blinked hard, and chewed his fingers. How Fleur stepped up to him, drew her knife. He smiled foolishly and asked her for supper. She reached forward and trimmed off a hank of his hair. Then she stalked from the house, leaving a taste of cold wind, and then chased Lazarre to the barn.

She made a black silhouette against the light from the door. Lazarre pressed against the wood of the walls, watching, hypnotized by the sight of Fleur's head and the quiet blade. He did not defend himself when she approached, reached for him, gently and efficiently cut bits of his hair, held his hands, one at a time, and trimmed the nails. She waved the razor-edged knife

1 **scheming** ['ski:mɪŋ] making sly plans – 3 **to strangle** to be killed by having a rope put around one's neck so one cannot breathe – 4 **deadfall** *here:* a hole – 17 **frigid** ['frɪdʒɪd] cold – 18 **pool** a type of billiards – 19 **cue stick** long, thin wooden stick used to hit the ball in billiards – **slush** melting snow – 22 **to ignite** to start burning – 25 **asked her for** asked her to stay for – **hank** loop, piece – 26 **to stalk** [stɔ:k] to move quietly – 31 **efficient** [ɪ'fɪʃənt] acting very effectively

before his eyes and swept a few eyelashes into a white square of flour sacking that she then carefully folded into her blouse.

For days after, Lazarre babbled and wept. Fleur was murdering him by use of bad medicine, he said. He showed his hand, the bite that Margaret had dealt him, and the dark streak from the wound, along his wrist and inching up his arm. He even used that bound hand to scratch his name from the treaty, but it did no good.

I figured that the two men were doomed at least three ways now. Margaret won the debate with her Catholic training and decided to damn her soul by taking up the ax, since no one else had destroyed her enemies. I begged her to wait for another week, all during which it snowed and thawed and snowed again. It took me that long to arrange the snare to my satisfaction, near Lazarre's shack, on a path both men took to town.

I set it out one morning before anyone stirred, and watched from an old pine twisted along the ground. I waited while the smoke rose in a silky feather from the tiny tin spout on Lazarre's roof. I had to sit half a day before Lazarre came outside, and even then it was just for wood, nowhere near the path. I had a hard time to keep my blood flowing, my stomach still. I ate a handful of dry berries Margaret had given me, and a bit of pounded meat. I doled it to myself and waited until finally Clarence showed. He walked the trail like a blind ghost and stepped straight into my noose.

It was perfect, or would have been if I had made the deadfall two inches wider, for in falling Clarence somehow managed to spread his legs and straddle the deep hole I'd cut. It had been invisible, covered with snow, and yet in one foot-pedaling instant, the certain knowledge of its construction sprang into Clarence's brain and told his legs to reach for the sides. I don't know how he did it, but there he was poised. I waited, did not show myself. The noose jerked enough to cut slightly into the fool's neck, a too-snug fit. He was spread-eagled and on tiptoe, his arms straight out. If he twitched a

1 **eyelash** one of a row of short hairs on the edge of the eyelid – **sacking** cloth used for making sacks – 3 **to babble** to talk in a confused way – 5 **to deal** *here:* to give – **wrist** [rɪst] the joint between the forearm and the hand – **to inch** to move very slowly – 8 **to figure** *(A.E. coll.)* to believe – **to be doomed** to be certain to be destroyed – 11 **to thaw** to become warm enough for snow to melt – 14 **to stir** to move – 15 **silky** soft, smooth and shiny like silk (seidig) – 16 **spout** *here:* chimney – 19 **pounded** crushed into a paste – 20 **to dole s.th. (out) to s.o.** to give s.th. to s.o. in small quantities – 21 **noose** [nu:s] a piece of rope that is tied into a circle – 24 **to straddle s.th.** to stand with one leg on each side of s.th. – 25 **instant** moment – 28 **to jerk** to pull suddenly and forcefully – 29 **spread-eagled** with arms and legs spread out

finger, lost the least control, even tried to yell, one foot would go, the noose constrict.

But Clarence did not move. I could see from behind my branches that he didn't even dare to change the expression on his face. His mouth stayed frozen in shock. Only his eyes shifted, darted fiercely and wildly, side to side, showing all the agitation he must not release, searching desperately for a means of escape. They focused only when I finally stepped toward him, quiet, from the pine.

We were in full view of Lazarre's house, face to face. I stood before the boy. Just a touch, a sudden kick, perhaps no more than a word, was all that it would take. But I looked into his eyes and saw the knowledge of his situation. Pity entered me. Even for Margaret's shame, I couldn't do the thing I might have done.

I turned away and left Morrissey still balanced on the ledge of snow.

What money I did have, I took to the trading store next day. I bought the best bonnet on the reservation. It was black as a coal scuttle, large, and shaped the same.

"It sets off my doe eyes," Margaret said and stared me down.

She wore it every day, and always to Mass. Not long before Lent and voices could be heard: "There goes Old Lady Coalbucket." Nonetheless, she was proud, and softening day by day, I could tell. By the time we got our foreheads crossed with ashes, she consented to be married.

"I hear you're thinking of exchanging the vows," said Father Damien as I shook his hand on our way out the door.

"I'm having relations with Margaret already," I told him, "that's the way we do things."

This had happened to him before, so he was not even stumped as to what remedy he should use.

"Make a confession, at any rate," he said, motioning us back into the church.

1 **to yell** to shout, to cry out loudly – 2 **to constrict** to squeeze tightly – 5 **to dart** to move suddenly and quickly – 6 **agitation** anxiety, worry, nervousness – **to release** [-s] to set free, to let go – 7 **to focus** to adjust the eyes so that you can see clearly what you want to look at – 14 **ledge** a small, narrow shelf – 16 **coal scuttle** a bucket for coal (it is specially shaped so that you can tip coal from it into a fire more easily) – 22 **to consent to s.th.** to agree to s.th. – 23 **vow** a solemn promise – **to exchange the vows** *here:* to get married (an allusion to the wedding ceremony) – 27 **to stump** to puzzle, to confuse – 28 **remedy** a cure – 29 **to motion** to indicate through a gesture that s.o. should move to a certain place

So I stepped into the little box and knelt. Father Damien slid aside the shadowy door. I told him what I had been doing with Margaret and he stopped me partway through.

"No more details. Pray to Our Lady."

"There is one more thing."

"Yes?"

"Clarence Morrissey, he wears a scarf to church around his neck each week. I snared him like a rabbit."

Father Damien let the silence fill him.

"And the last thing," I went on, "I stole the wire from your piano."

The silence spilled over into my stall, and I was held in its grip until the priest spoke.

"Discord is hateful to God. You have offended his ear." Almost as an afterthought, Damien added, "And his commandment. The violence among you must cease."

"You can have the wire back," I said. I had used only one long strand. I also agreed that I would never use my snares on humans, an easy promise. Lazarre was already caught.

Just two days later, while Margaret and I stood with Lulu and her mother inside the trading store, Lazarre entered, gesturing, his eyes rolled to the skull. He stretched forth his arm and pointed along its deepest black vein and dropped his jaw wide. Then he stepped backward into a row of traps that the trader had set to show us how they worked. Fleur's eye lit, her white scarf caught the sun as she turned. All the whispers were true. Fleur had scratched Lazarre's figure into a piece of birchbark, drawn his insides, and rubbed a bit of rouge up his arm until the red stain reached his heart. There was no sound as he fell, no cry, no word, and the traps of all types that clattered down around his body jumped and met for a long time, snapping air.

13 **discord** ['– –] 1. a combination of musical notes which sounds unattractive, 2. disagreement and quarrelling among people – 21 **skull** the bone of one's head which encloses the brain

Biographical Notes

Louise Erdrich was born in Little Falls, Minnesota, in 1954. She is of German-American and Chippewa descent and an enrolled member of the Turtle Mountain Band of Chippewa.

Her parents were teachers at the Wahpeton Indian Boarding School in North Dakota, where she attended primary and secondary school before studying at Dartmouth College, New Hampshire, from 1972 to 1976. Having graduated, she returned to North Dakota to teach poetry. After attending Johns Hopkins University, Maryland, in 1978, she received a degree in creative writing.

In her relatively short but highly successful career as a writer and editor, Louise Erdrich has received a large number of literary awards. She has edited The Circle, *the Boston Indian Council Newspaper, has published poetry (*Jacklight, *1984), short stories and novels. The* Sunday Times *called her "one of the most exciting and surprising novelists writing in English [who] tells of America's dispossessed, her Indian forefathers, in a compassion untainted by sentimentality. And she has given the Chippewas of North Dakota a lasting place in fiction."*

Love Medicine, *her first novel, appeared in 1984,* The Beet Queen *in 1986, and* Tracks *was published in 1988. Louise Erdrich lives in New Hampshire with her husband Michael Dorris, also an author, and their six children.*

The story printed here was first published in Harper's Magazine *and later integrated, in slightly modified form, in the novel* Tracks.

Gerald Vizenor

Marleen American Horse

> "The trick is in what one emphasizes," he said. "We either make ourselves miserable, or we make ourselves strong. The amount of work is the same."
>
> CARLOS CASTANEDA *Journey to Ixtlan*

The United States Army Corps of Engineers contracted for the construction of the Garrison Dam to hold back the Missouri River in North Dakota. Elbowoods, a small tribal village, the home and birthplace of Marleen American Horse, fell beneath the new flood, the federal creation of Lake Sakakawea, on the Fort Berthold Reservation.

Marleen American Horse came to Minneapolis with a single change of clothes in a brown paper sack and an old reservation allotment map showing her place on the earth before the flood. Not before the great mythical tribal flood which balanced the sacred earth, but before the flood of white men and their pleasure boats.

She even married a white man after the flood, a truck driver who turned violent toward women when he was drunk, which was three times a week on schedule, and he expressed his love for her on the same schedule. Three mixedblood children later, two dark and one light, and a decade since the flood, she traveled to the same bars to be with the man who abused her for her sins. She became a despondent alcoholic.

In drunkenness she gave herself to evil lust and the hostilities of white men who loved to abuse tribal women. Morning after morning, she recognized her desolation and personal destruction. Her children hungered alone at night in a cold apartment. Drinking was all she could do to ease the guilt and pain from drinking. She smiled as best she could in the late mornings with

1 **to contract** ['––] to make a legal or written agreement – 2 **dam** barrier built to keep back water – 4 **federal** of the U.S. government – 7 **allotment** small area of land set aside for s.o.'s use – 13 **on schedule** ['ʃedjʊl; A.E.: 'sk–] at the expected or planned time – 14 **decade** ['dekeɪd] period of ten years – 15 **to abuse** [ə'bju:z] to treat in a bad way – 16 **despondent** [dɪs–] having or showing no more hope – 17 **hostilities** [–'–––] acts of fighting, opposition – 19 **desolation** state of being sad and lonely

numb lips, and turned under the memories of her sacred tribal past. But she would not give up her translated tribal name.

she learned english
without a winter coat
in a cold place for sacred names
milking cows
on federal labor farms
for another race

her brown feet
breaking through her red charity shoes

squaw for the soldiers
who bought her another drink

white city soldiers
cursing her dark eyes at night

mauling her breasts for the cavalry
without a name

she was down
in a civilization she never understood
living forever

when the soldiers fell
one by one at the winter bar
she raised the sacred flag of her people
lifting with the eagles
dreaming
her children were coming home

Marleen American Horse lost her children. Welfare workers placed them in foster homes. One winter morning when she returned from drinking, walking through the fresh snow, she learned that she had been evicted from her apartment. The locks were changed. There was an eviction notice on the door. Her television set, her clothes, memorabilia, and the reservation map

1 **numb** [nʌm] unable to feel or move – **to turn under** to try to forget, to wipe out – 5 **sacred names** tribal names – 10 **charity shoes** shoes given to her by an organization helping the poor – 15 **to maul** [ɔ:] to hurt by brutal handling – 23 **to lift** *here:* to rise high in the air – **the eagle** sacred bird for Native Americans (whose feathers were used in many tribal ceremonies) – 26 **welfare worker** social worker – 27 **foster home** home for children who have lost their parents – 28 **to be evicted** to be turned out of a house etc. by force of law (*n.* eviction) – 30 **memorabilia** things reminding s.o. of an event, another person etc.

showing her birthplace, the few objects remaining in her name, were gone, stolen or given away.

She slumped in the snow on the outside stairs and began to weep and wail for her children and her losses to white men and alcoholism. She wanted nothing more than to be loved in a cold and insensitive world. Her weaknesses were shunned on the street. She slipped into a telephone booth, shivering from the cold, and called a welfare worker who in turn referred her to the Waite Neighborhood House on Park Avenue in Minneapolis.

"Good morning, Waite House," said the receptionist.

"This is my last dime to call ..."

"Who would you like to speak to?"

"My children are gone ..."

"One minute please."

The call was transferred to the tribal advocate at the Neighborhood House. He was drinking coffee in the kitchen of the old mansion. He was a mixed-blood writer who became an advocate for tribal people in trouble. Whatever the reason, he announced several times a week in tribal drinking and eating places on the urban reservation that he would argue and represent the expressed needs of tribal people. He answered the telephone call in his office.

"Tell me trouble with a smile," he said.

"I have to stop drinking ... My children are gone and this is my last dime, please don't hang up ... I have to stop drinking. I am cold, someone took my winter coat last night," she told. Even her voice shivered from the cold.

"Where are you?" asked the advocate.

"In a booth by the Band Box on Tenth Avenue near Chicago," she said.

"Who are you?"

"Marleen ... Marleen American Horse Peterson."

The tribal advocate told her to wait in the telephone booth until he arrived. He drove to the intersection, doubtful that she would be calling with her last dime and with no winter clothes. But she was there and what she said was the truth. She huddled in the front seat of the car, shivering from the cold and trembling from her need for alcohol.

3 **to slump** to fall, to drop – **to wail for s.o. or s.th.** to complain in a loud voice – 5 **insensitive** [–'–––] without feeling – 6 **to be shunned** to pass unnoticed, to be avoided – **booth** telephone box – 10 **dime** coin worth 10 cents – 14 **advocate** ['ædvəkət] s.o. who speaks or acts in support of a person or a group of people – 15 **mansion** large and stately house – 25 **Chicago** Chicago Street in Minneapolis – 29 **intersection** ['––––] *(A.E.)* crossing – 31 **to huddle** *here:* to curl up

She sat in the kitchen of the Neighborhood House drinking black coffee, eating rolls, and retelling stories about her children, her birthplace and losses, and her last dime. The muscles on her face twitched when she spoke. Her lips were swollen. She was hesitant in her gestures, but she said she had to keep talking to keep from breaking down in tears.

"Nothing is left for me now."

"There never was anything, except, perhaps, a fantastic lover now and then," he said, shrugging his shoulders and smiling. He was sitting on his desk looking out the window while he sipped his coffee and waited for her response to his humor. His manner was affectionate and direct, but he spoke in a firm voice, harsh at times, showing humor and provoking arguments at the same time. He forced tribal people to speak in anger, to show their rage. An obligation, he once told his friends, to express fear and courage, the hard lessons he learned from his own poor childhood. He refused to accept dependencies in tribal people. He would sooner insult and provoke tribal people than to encourage dependencies. As a tribal advocate, he was loved and hated, but he was never mistrusted.

"But this drinking is killing me ..."

"Sometimes we are worth killing," he said.

"My children are gone," she pleaded.

"Change comes from within," he said, watching her face muscles as he spoke. "Through your dark eyes, and when you have dark skin the change is never simple. ... White people think we are simple, simple like children and animals, pets, and we learn their simple words for our own problems and failures. ... So now, this morning, before you stop drinking, you do want to stop drinking, right?"

"Yes, please help me do that."

"No one else will help you, but the first thing to do now is to unwind the tribe from the white words we have become. ... Not forever, because white people are humorous and pleasant at times, but now we want to find out what those white words about your problem mean in your head. ..."

"Can you commit me as an alcoholic?"

3 **to twitch** to make a sudden, often uncontrollable movement – 4 **swollen** [əʊ] having grown bigger than normal – **hesitant** slow to act – **gesture** movement of the body, usually the hands, to help express meaning – 8 **to shrug one's shoulders** to raise the shoulders slightly in order to show doubt or indifference – 9 **to sip** to drink taking only a small quantity at a time – 10 **affectionate** friendly, showing love – 11 **harsh** cruel – **at times** sometimes, every now and then – 12 **rage** great anger – 28 **to unwind** [ʌn'waɪnd] *here:* to free – 32 **to commit** *here:* to hand over to an institution

"No problem, but not for openers. ... Listen now, drink your coffee and listen, white words have become part of the problem, white expectations, because we are held down, stuck in our own problems, through the language of white people. ..."

"I have a terrible headache."

"Close your eyes while you listen and let your stomach go, relax your stomach, you are sitting too tense," he said, touching her shoulders. "Now just let your stomach go and let your legs go, take a short nap now while you listen for a few more minutes. ... We are living in an impossible dream as winners and failures. ... We are taught to be failures for the winners and then we must be grateful to those who are pledged to help us through the problems defined in white words. ... We should all be at war with words, word wars, because we have been historical losers.

"We are treated like children in a new school on the first morning of classes, words are like prisons then, new controls, learning the definitions of tribute to the teachers. And we are taught to praise those who detain and define us in simple words, disagreement is defined as being a loser, and when we speak our own language, not tribal languages now, but the languages of our hearts and our experiences, the tongue of our hearts, we are shunned or punished for speaking without manners.

"But you are not a child, you are not made out of white words, you are Marleen American Horse, a beautiful tribal drunk, a special sort of alcoholic from the reservation, a troubled visitor in the cities, wandering and warning the people about the coming doom, becoming the doom, you pass greetings from the urban reservation. ...When you accept the worst words from drinking places in white minds you become dependent on the definitions, and dependent on the word cures. Are you a white person?"

"No, of course not, you can see that."

"Then how come you have a white problem?"

"What white problem?" she asked.

"Drunken Indian."

"But I want my three children back. ... I keep trying to stop drinking, honest, this morning, honest. ..."

"No money is all that stops you now," he said.

1 **not for openers** not as the first thing – 3 **to hold down** not to allow to make progress – 6 **to let go** *here:* to relax – 7 **tense** not relaxed – 8 **a nap** a short sleep, usually during the day – 11 **to be pledged** *here:* to promise – 16 **tribute** expression of praise, thanks – **to detain** to keep like a prisoner – 24 **doom** a terrible fate – 27 **cure** substance or treatment which makes s.o. healthy again

"Well, that's why I'm here, for someone to help me."

"The reason you are here makes no difference to me," he said, lighting a hand-rolled cigarette and offering it to her. He then rolled a second cigarette while he continued talking. "But listen, do you think people can help you to stop drinking?"

"Well, yes, someone can," she anwered.

"Who will help? Name a person or place now."

"Some agencies."

"Which ones will help you?"

"The ones for drinking," she said.

"But those agencies speak white words about your problem. … The cause of the problem is not the cure in words unless you are a trickster or a warrior. … But you are a drunk, in white words you are an alcoholic, and a good one because you have lost everything, and we all know that people from reservations have drinking problems in white languages. Can the words that define your problem become the cure for your problem, cures in the same words that created the problem?"

"What are you talking about?"

"Word wars."

"What does that mean?" she asked.

"Will words change you?"

"Well, no, not to change, not words. …"

"Then how come you have been sitting there, smoking a hand-rolled cigarette, drinking coffee and listening to me tell you that I love you, I love you too much to deceive you. … This is no cure in words, answers are not cures, words are not cures, ceremonies are cures, but not oaths and promises and the bullshit language of cures. … These are dependencies. Word cures are like eating menus for dinner and wondering why our children still hunger. … Word cures cause internal word wars. … Words have power when words are not over the counter cures."

"But what can I do, no one cares."

"Care for yourself. … If you must drink, then drink in good humor, drink with the courage of a warrior and feel good, but never drink as a problem. Caring for yourself is not drinking like a white word problem and feeling guilty about it later."

8 **agency** organization – 12 **trickster** a culture hero of Indian tribes – 25 **to deceive s.o.** [dɪ'si:v] to cheat – 26 **ceremonies** *here:* tribal ceremonies – **oath** [əʊθ] solemn declaration that s.th. is true – 27 **bullshit** *(sl.)* vulgar expression used to show disapproval – 30 **over the counter** simply to be bought

"I am afraid, and I need a drink."

"Then you must learn how to drink without guilt," he said in a softer tone of voice. "But if you were free from guilt then you would not need to drink for any reason. … What I am trying to say like a trickster, the sad news, the bottom line, is that there are few people who will help you."

"But you will."

"Here are the choices this morning," he said in a more businesslike tone of voice. "Look at it this way, there are three choices for now: one, you can come home with me and I will take care of you and then you can come to work with me and learn how to help others with their drinking problem, so that you can cure yourself by making other people feel guilty.

"Two, we can try to find an agency or hospital to receive you for treatment as an alcoholic. You can take the cure if someone will take you.

"Three, I can sign a complaint and have you committed to a sophisticated drunk tank for six months where they may or may not help you. … Which is it this morning?"

"Commit me."

"No," he said.

"But I don't have any money or clothes, nothing."

"Money is not the problem," he said, opening a large book containing a list of social service agencies in the state. "We can find the money, but first let's call every agency in this book, every agency in the city, and you listen in on the extension while I tell them about you and what your problem is and then you will see who will help you. … My guess is that every agency will first make an excuse that they can't help for some technical reason and then refer you to another agency. … Perpetual referral is a guiding principle in social services to the poor. The idea is to keep poor people, and people with problems, running from agency to agency on referral until they get mean or tired and stop asking. Agencies are made out of words and word cures and referrals are the best cures they know."

The tribal advocate called several agencies during the morning. Not one of them could help and all of them referred the client to another place. Marleen American Horse listened on the extension to the conversations. In the beginning she was embarrassed to hear people talking about her, but then she became depressed and discouraged. Late in the afternoon, when the advo-

5 **bottom line** the final result, basic truth – 14 **sophisticated** highly developed – 15 **drunk tank** *(sl.)* help centre for alcoholics – 22 **to listen in on the extension** auf dem Nebenanschluß mithören – 26 **perpetual** never-ending – 28 **mean** humble, humiliated – 34 **to be embarrassed** to feel awkward, ashamed

cate had called the last of the agencies, her depression disappeared in sudden bursts of laughter. She smiled and laughed through the last word referral cures over the telephone.

"This is where we started," said the advocate.

"But not like this morning when I called," she said.

"Which is it now?"

"Thank you for the offer, but I would not feel good going home with you. I would feel in the way and like trouble, you know, so I guess you should commit me. …"

"No, not unless you're drunk."

"No, no more drinking," she said.

The advocate, the tribal trickster and realist, took a business card with his name and two telephone numbers printed on it and taped two dimes to the front. "This," he said, handing the card to her, "is your commitment ticket. … When you get drunk again, call me at any time at either of these numbers and tell me where you are drinking and I will have you committed."

The advocate supplied her with clothing, a winter coat, a room with the rent paid for one month, cash to live for two weeks, which was drawn from a special fund to assist tribal people. Then he took her to dinner. The two of them talked about the weather, her birthplace before the flood, their children, their travels, old memories, dreams, fantasies, love and being loved, and then she asked him to leave her at the same telephone booth she used to call him in the morning.

She smiled when she left the car and waited near the telephone booth until he drove away. The advocate never heard from her again.

17 **to supply s.o. with s.th.** to give s.o. s.th. – 18 **to draw** *here:* to take – 19 **to assist** to help

Biographical Notes

Gerald Vizenor, a mixed-blood Chippewa (or Anishinabe) was born in Minneapolis, Minnesota, in 1934. He experienced a particularly hard childhood there. His father, half Anishinabe, half white, had left the White Earth Reservation in northern Minnesota for the city, where he was killed by a mugger when Gerald was only twenty months old. Gerald and his mother then had to live in poverty until she remarried. Eight years later, however, she deserted her family. Gerald continued to live with his stepfather, who – within six months – was killed in an accident leaving the boy all alone again.

"Given this childhood, filled with desertion and violent deaths, it is not surprising that Vizenor developed a bizarre and bloody view of the universe. Rather than reacting with despair, however, Vizenor has joined the fight against absurdity and injustice with the elan of the Anishinabe trickster Wenebojo." (Alan R. Velie, Four American Indian Literary Masters, *Norman, 1982, p. 125).*

In spite of the events of his childhood, Gerald Vizenor has had a very successful professional career. He attended New York University and received a B.A. degree from the University of Minnesota. He has held various posts including that of Director of the American Indian Employment and Guidance Center in Minneapolis. He is currently Professor of Native American Studies at the University of California (Berkeley).

His book Earthdivers: Tribal Narratives on Mixed Descent *(1981) looks at the plight of mixed-blood Indians living in urban areas. The same theme – life on the urban reservation – reappears in "Marleen American Horse," a partly authentic story taken from a number of sketches –* Wordarrows: Indians and Whites in the New Fur Trade *(1978) – that are based on Vizenor's own experiences as a social worker. This collection gives "a highly revealing picture of a ghetto people – their power and dignity, flaws and foibles, and, above all, their essential humanity." (Velie, p. 126).*

In addition, Vizenor has published poetry, reviews, articles, children's stories, a quite sophisticated novel, Darkness in Saint Louis Bearheart *(1978), and narratives on Minnesota Indians.*

Mary Whitebird

Ta-Na-E-Ka

As my birthday drew closer, I had awful nightmares about it. I was reaching the age at which all Kaw Indians had to participate in Ta-Na-E-Ka. Well, not all Kaws. Many of the younger families on the reservation were beginning to give up the old customs. But my grandfather, Amos Deer Leg, was devoted to tradition. He still wore handmade beaded moccasins instead of shoes, and kept his iron-gray hair in tight braids. He could speak English, but he spoke it only with white men. With his family he used a Sioux dialect.

Grandfather was one of the last living Indians (he died in 1953 when he was 81) who actually fought against the U.S. Cavalry. Not only did he fight, he was wounded in a skirmish at Rose Creek – a famous encounter in which the celebrated Kaw chief Flat Nose lost his life. At the time, my grandfather was only 11 years old.

Eleven was a magic word among the Kaws. It was the time of Ta-Na-E-Ka, the "flowering of adulthood". It was the age, my grandfather informed us hundreds of times, "when a boy could prove himself to be a warrior and a girl took the first steps to womanhood."

"I don't want to be a warrior," my cousin, Roger Deer Leg, confided to me. "I'm going to become an accountant."

"None of the other tribes make girls go through the endurance ritual," I complained to my mother.

"It won't be as bad as you think, Mary," my mother said, ignoring my protests. "Once you've gone through it, you'll certainly never forget it. You'll be proud."

I even complained to my teacher, Mrs. Richardson, feeling that, as a white woman, she would side with me.

2 **Kaw** also *Kansa;* a plains tribe of North American Indians who lived in what is now known as the state of Kansas – 4 **to be devoted to** to be loyal to, to stick to – 5 **beaded** decorated with small balls made of glass or wood (perlenbesetzt) – 6 **braids** Zöpfe – 7 **Sioux** [su:] group of Indian tribes of the Northern plains – 10 **skirmish** a minor battle – **encounter** meeting; fight – 14 **flowering of adulthood** beginning of life as an adult – 15 **warrior** fighter – 17 **to confide s.th. to s.o.** to tell s.o. a secret – 18 **accountant** Buchhalter – 19 **endurance** ability to stand pain or hardship for a length of time

She didn't. "All of us have rituals of one kind or another," Mrs. Richardson said. "And look at it this way: How many girls have the opportunity to compete on equal terms with boys? Don't look down on your heritage."

Heritage, indeed? I had no intention of living on a reservation for the rest of my life. I was a good student. I loved school. My fantasies were about knights in armor and fair ladies in flowing gowns, being saved from dragons. It never once occurred to me that being an Indian was exciting.

But I've always thought that the Kaw were the originators of the women's liberation movement. No other Indian tribe – and I've spent half a lifetime researching the subject – treated women more "equally" than the Kaw. Unlike most of the subtribes of the Sioux Nation, the Kaw allowed men and women to eat together. And hundreds of years before we were "acculturated," a Kaw woman had the right to refuse a prospective husband even if her father arranged the match.

The wisest women (generally wisdom was equated with age) often sat in tribal councils. Furthermore, most Kaw legends revolve around "Good Woman," a kind of super-squaw, a Joan of Arc of the high plains. Good Woman led Kaw warriors into battle after battle from which they always seemed to emerge victorious.

And girls as well as boys were required to undergo Ta-Na-E-Ka.

The actual ceremony varied from tribe to tribe, but since the Indians' life on the plains was dedicated to survival, Ta-Na-E-Ka was a test of survival.

"Endurance is the loftiest virtue of the Indian," my grandfather explained. "To survive, we must endure. When I was a boy, Ta-Na-E-Ka was more than the mere symbol it is now. We were painted white with the juice of a sacred herb and sent naked into the wilderness without so much as a knife. We couldn't return until the white had worn off. It took almost 18 days, and during that time we had to stay alive, trapping food, eating insects and roots and berries, and watching out for enemies. And we did have enemies – both the white soldiers and the Omaha warriors, who were always trying to cap-

3 **on equal terms with** under the same conditions – **heritage** ['herɪtɪdʒ] traditions, values, etc. handed down to us by our forefathers – 6 **armor** metal protection worn by a knight in a fight – **dragon** Drache – 12 **to be acculturated** to come into contact, to be influenced by another culture – 13 **prospective** future – 14 **match** *here:* the bringing together of two people in marriage – 15 **to be equated with** to be considered the same as – 16 **to revolve around** *here:* to centre on, to deal with – 17 **Joan of Arc** French heroine who defeated the English at Orleans in 1429; later burned for witchcraft – 19 **to emerge** [ɪ'mɜːdʒ] to come out – 23 **lofty** noble, most important – 25 **mere** no more than, only – **sacred** holy – 26 **herb** plant – 30 **the Omaha** ['əʊməˌhɑː] tribe of Indians in northeastern Nebraska

ture Kaw boys and girls undergoing their endurance test. It was an exciting time."

"What happened if you couldn't make it?" Roger asked. He was born only three days after I was, and we were being trained for Ta-Na-E-Ka together. I was happy to know he was frightened too.

"Many didn't return," Grandfather said. "Only the strongest and shrewdest. Mothers were not allowed to weep over those who didn't return. If a Kaw couldn't survive, he or she wasn't worth weeping over. It was our way."

"What a lot of hooey," Roger whispered. "I'd give anything to get out of it."

"I don't see how we have any choice," I replied.

Roger gave my arm a little squeeze. "Well, it's only five days."

Five days! Maybe it was better than being painted white and set out naked for 18 days. But not much better.

We were to be sent, barefoot and in bathing suits, into the woods. Even our very traditional parents put their foot down when Grandfather suggested we go naked. For five days we'd have to live off the land, keeping warm as best we could, getting food where we could. It was May, but on the northernmost reaches of the Missouri River the days were still chilly and the nights were fiercely cold.

Grandfather was in charge of the month's training for Ta-Na-E-Ka. One day he caught a grasshopper and demonstrated how to pull its legs and wings off in one flick of the fingers and how to swallow it.

I felt sick, and Roger turned green. "It's a darn good thing it's 1947," I told Roger teasingly. "You'd make a terrible warrior." Roger just grimaced.

I knew one thing. This particular Kaw Indian girl wasn't going to swallow a grasshopper no matter how hungry she got. And then I had an idea. Why hadn't I thought of it before? It would have saved nights of bad dreams about squooshy grasshoppers.

I headed straight for my teacher's house. "Mrs. Richardson," I said, "would you lend me five dollars?"

"Five dollars!" she exclaimed. "What for?"

"You remember the ceremony I talked about?"

"Ta-Na-E-Ka. Of course. Your parents have written me and asked me to excuse you from school so you can participate in it."

6 **shrewd** [ʃru:d] clever – 9 **hooey** ['hu:ɪ] *(A.E. sl.)* nonsense – 12 **squeeze** act of pressing s.th. or s.o. – 21 **to be in charge of** responsible for – 24 **darn** *(sl.)* damned – 25 **to tease s.o.** to make fun of s.o., to mock s.o. – **to grimace** to pull a face (*e.g.* to express pain) – 29 **squooshy** ['skwʊʃɪ] soft, slimy

"Well, I need some things for the ceremony," I replied, in a half truth. "I don't want to ask my parents for the money."

"It's not a crime to borrow money, Mary. But how can you pay it back?"

"I'll baby-sit for you 10 times."

"That's more than fair," she said, going to her purse and handing me a crisp new five-dollar bill. I'd never had that much money at once.

"I'm happy to know the money's going to be put to a good use," Mrs. Richardson said.

A few days later, the ritual began with a long speech from my grandfather about how we had reached the age of decision, how we now had to fend for ourselves and prove that we could survive the most horrendous of ordeals. All the friends and relatives who gathered at our house for dinner made jokes about their own Ta-Na-E-Ka experiences. They all advised us to fill up now, since for the next five days we'd be gorging ourselves on crickets. Neither Roger nor I was very hungry. "I'll probably laugh about this when I'm an accountant," Roger said, trembling.

"Are you trembling?" I asked.

"What do you think?"

"I'm happy to know boys tremble too." I said.

At six the next morning we kissed our parents and went off to the woods. "Which side do you want?" Roger asked. According to the rules, Roger and I would stake out "territories" in separate areas of the woods and we weren't to communicate during the entire ordeal.

"I'll go toward the river, if it's OK with you," I said.

"Sure," Roger answered. "What difference does it make?"

To me, it made a lot of difference. There was a marina a few miles up the river and there were boats moored there. At least, I hoped so. I figured that a boat was a better place to sleep than under a pile of leaves.

"Why do you keep holding your head?" Roger asked.

"Oh, nothing. Just nervous," I told him. Actually, I was afraid I'd lose the five-dollar bill, which I had tucked into my hair with a bobby pin. As we came to a fork in the trail, Roger shook my hand. "Good luck, Mary."

6 **crisp** newly made and therefore still firm – **bill** *(A.E.)* banknote – 10 **to fend for oneself** to look after oneself without any help from others – 11 **horrendous** terrible – **ordeal** [ɔ:'di:l] test of character and endurance, unpleasant experience – 14 **to gorge oneself** to eat greedily – **cricket** a small jumping insect (Grille) – 22 **to stake out** to mark an area that one claims for oneself – 23 **entire** [en'taɪə] whole – 26 **marina** [mə'ri:nə] harbour for small boats – 27 **to moor** to tie a ship to land – 31 **to tuck** *here:* to fix – **bobby pin** hair clip

"N'ko-n'ta," I said. It was the Kaw word for *courage*.

The sun was shining and it was warm, but my bare feet began to hurt immediately. I spied one of the berry bushes Grandfather had told us about. "You're lucky," he had said. "The berries are ripe in the spring, and they are delicious and nourishing." They were orange and fat and I popped one into my mouth.

Argh! I spat it out. It was awful and bitter, and even grasshoppers were probably better-tasting, although I never intended to find out.

I sat down to rest my feet. A rabbit hopped out from under the berry bush. He nuzzled the berry I'd spat out and ate it. He picked another one and ate that too. He liked them. He looked at me, twitching his nose. I watched a redheaded woodpecker bore into an elm tree, and I caught a glimpse of a civet cat waddling through some twigs. All of a sudden I realized I was no longer frightened. Ta-Na-E-Ka might be more fun than I'd anticipated. I got up and headed toward the marina.

"Not one boat," I said to myself dejectedly. But the restaurant on the shore, "Ernie's Riverside," was open. I walked in, feeling silly in my bathing suit. The man at the counter was big and tough-looking. He wore a sweatshirt with the words "Fort Sheridan, 1944," and he had only three fingers on one of his hands. He asked me what I wanted.

"A hamburger and a milk shake," I said, holding the five-dollar bill in my hand so he'd know I had money.

"That's a pretty heavy breakfast, honey," he said.

"That's what I always have for breakfast," I lied.

"Forty-five cents," he said, bringing me the food. (Back in 1947, hamburgers were 25 cents and milk shakes were 20 cents.) "Delicious," I thought, "Better 'n grasshoppers – and Grandfather never once mentioned that I couldn't eat hamburgers."

While I was eating, I had a grand idea. Why not sleep in the restaurant? I went to the ladies' room and made sure the window was unlocked. Then I went back outside and played along the river bank, watching the water birds and trying to identify each one. I planned to look for a beaver dam the next day.

5 **delicious** [dɪ'lɪʃəs] tasting very good – 10 **to nuzzle** ['nʌzl] to touch with the nose – 11 **to twitch** to move quickly and without meaning to – 12 **woodpecker** Specht – 13 **civet cat** *here:* skunk – **to waddle** ['wɒdl] to walk like a duck – 14 **to anticipate** [æn'tɪsɪpeɪt] to expect – 16 **dejected** disappointed, sad, miserable – 27 **better'n** *(sl.)* better than – 32 **beaver** Biber

The restaurant closed at sunset, and I watched the three-fingered man drive away. Then I climbed in the unlocked window. There was a night-light on, so I didn't turn on any lights. But there was a radio on the counter. I turned it on to a music program. It was warm in the restaurant, and I was hungry. I helped myself to a glass of milk and a piece of pie, intending to keep a list of what I'd eaten so I could leave money. I also planned to get up early, sneak out through the window, and head for the woods before the three-fingered man returned. I turned off the radio, wrapped myself in the man's apron, and, in spite of the hardness of the floor, fell asleep.

"What the heck are you doing here, kid?"

It was the man's voice.

It was morning. I'd overslept. I was scared.

"Hold it, kid. I just wanna know what you're doing here. You lost? You must be from the reservation. Your folks must be worried sick about you. Do they have a phone?"

"Yes, yes," I answered. "But don't call them."

I was shivering. The man, who told me his name was Ernie, made me a cup of hot chocolate while I explained about Ta-Na-E-Ka.

"Darnedest thing I ever heard," he said, when I was through. "Lived next to the reservation all my life and this is the first I've heard of Ta-Na whatever-you-call-it." He looked at me, all goosebumps in my bathing suit. "Pretty silly thing to do to a kid," he muttered.

That was just what I'd been thinking for months, but when Ernie said it, I became angry. "No, it isn't silly. It's a custom of the Kaw. We've been doing this for hundreds of years. My mother und my grandfather and everybody in my family went through this ceremony. It's why the Kaw are great warriors."

"OK, great warrior," Ernie chuckled, "suit yourself. And, if you want to stick around, it's OK with me." Ernie went to the broom closet and tossed me a bundle. "That's the lost-and-found closet," he said. "Stuff people left on boats. Maybe there's something to keep you warm."

The sweater fitted loosely, but it felt good. I felt good. And I'd found a new friend. Most important, I was surviving Ta-Na-E-Ka.

5 **to intend** to plan – 10 **what the heck** *(sl.)* what on earth – 13 **wanna** *(sl.)* want to – 14 **folks** [fəʊks] *(coll.)* family, relatives – 19 **darnedest** *(coll.)* most remarkable – **through** *here:* finished – 21 **goosebumps** small bumps which appear on the skin when one is cold – 22 **to mutter** to speak in a low voice or unclearly – 27 **to chuckle** to laugh quietly – **suit yourself** do as you please – 28 **closet** ['klɒsɪt] small room for storing things – **to toss** to throw through the air

My grandfather had said the experience would be filled with adventure, and I was having my fill. And, Grandfather had never said we couldn't accept hospitality.

I stayed at Ernie's Riverside for the entire period. In the mornings I went into the woods and watched the animals and picked flowers for each of the tables in Ernie's. I had never felt better. I was up early enough to watch the sun rise on the Missouri, and I went to bed after it set. I ate everything I wanted – insisting that Ernie take all my money for the food. "I'll keep this in trust for you, Mary," Ernie promised, "in case you are ever desperate for five dollars." (He did too, but that's another story.)

I was sorry when the five days were over. I'd enjoyed every minute with Ernie. He taught me how to make western omelets and to make Chili Ernie Style (still one of my favorite dishes). And I told Ernie all about the legends of the Kaw. I hadn't realized I knew so much about my people. But Ta-Na-E-Ka was over, and as I approached my house, at about 9 : 30 in the evening, I became nervous all over again. What if Grandfather asked me about the berries and the grasshoppers? And my feet were hardly cut. I hadn't lost a pound and my hair was combed.

"They'll be so happy to see me," I told myself hopefully, "that they won't ask too many questions."

I opened the door. My grandfather was in the front room. He was wearing the ceremonial beaded deerskin shirt which had belonged to *his* grandfather. "N'g'da'ma," he said. "Welcome back."

I embraced my parents warmly, letting go only when I saw my cousin Roger sprawled on the couch. His eyes were red and swollen. He'd lost weight. His feet were an unsightly mass of blood and blisters, and he was moaning: "I made it, see. I made it. I'm a warrior. A warrior."

My grandfather looked at me strangely. I was clean, obviously well-fed, and radiantly healthy. My parents got the message. My uncle and aunt gazed at me with hostility.

Finally my grandfather asked, "What did you eat to keep you so well?"

I sucked in my breath and blurted out the truth: "Hamburgers and milk shakes."

2 **to have one's fill** to have as much as one needs to be satisfied – 3 **hospitality** [– –'– – –] helpfulness, friendliness – 12 **western omelet** an omelet made with ham, green pepper (Paprika) and onions – **chili** chili con carne, a famous Mexican dish – 25 **to sprawl** to lie with arms and legs outstretched – 26 **blisters** Blasen – 27 **to moan** to make a low sound of pain – 29 **radiant** shining, bright – 30 **hostility** anger, unfriendliness – 32 **to blurt out s.th.** to suddenly tell s.th. which was intended to be kept secret

"Hamburgers!" my grandfather growled.

"Milk shakes!" Roger moaned.

"You didn't say we *had* to eat grasshoppers," I said sheepishly.

"Tell us all about your Ta-Na-E-Ka," my grandfather commanded.

I told them everything, from borrowing the five dollars, to Ernie's kindness, to observing the beaver.

"That's not what I trained you for," my grandfather said sadly.

I stood up. "Grandfather, I learned that Ta-Na-E-Ka *is* important. I didn't think so during training. I was scared stiff of it. I handled it my way. And I learned I had nothing to be afraid of. There's no reason in 1947 to eat grasshoppers when you can eat a hamburger."

I was inwardly shocked at my own audacity. But I liked it. "Grandfather, I'll bet you never ate one of those rotten berries yourself."

Grandfather laughed! He laughed aloud! My mother and father and aunt and uncle were all dumbfounded. Grandfather never laughed. Never.

"Those berries – they are terrible," Grandfather admitted. "I could never swallow them. I found a dead deer on the first day of my Ta-Na-E-Ka – shot by a soldier, probably – and he kept my belly full for the entire period of the test!“

Grandfather stopped laughing. "We should send you out again," he said.

I looked at Roger. "You're pretty smart, Mary," Roger groaned. "I'd never have thought of what you did."

"Accountants just have to be good at arithmetic," I said comfortably. "I'm terrible at arithmetic."

Roger tried to smile, but couldn't. My grandfather called me to him. "You should have done what your cousin did. But I think you are more alert to what is happening to our people today than we are. I think you would have passed the test under any circumstances, in any time. Somehow, you know how to exist in a world that wasn't made for Indians. I don't think you're going to have any trouble surviving."

Grandfather wasn't entirely right. But I'll tell about that another time.

1 **to growl** [graʊl] to make a low, threatening sound – 3 **sheepish** puzzled, ashamed (after doing s.th. stupid) – 9 **to be scared stiff** to be very much afraid – 12 **audacity** [ɔ:'dæsɪtɪ] boldness – 15 **to be dumbfounded** [dʌm'faʊndɪd] to be so astonished that one cannot speak – 21 **to groan** to moan – 26 **to be alert to s.th.** [ə'lɜ:t] to be fully aware of s.th.

Biographical Notes

"Mary Whitebird" is the pseudonym of a writer who has long had an interest in the life of the American Indian in the late 20th century. We asked the author's agents for biographical material and received this statement by Mary Whitebird:

"Mary Whitebird" is the pen name of a very private writer and film-maker who was born in Arizona, spent time on a reservation, and received an Emmy nomination for a network documentary on the problems of Indians.

DO YOU KNOW PONS?